SCAREDY CAT

JAMES PATTERSON
and Chris Grabenstein

ILLUSTRATED BY JOHN HERZOG

1 3 5 7 9 10 8 6 4 2

Young Arrow
20 Vauxhall Bridge Road
London SW1V 2SA

Young Arrow is part of the Penguin Random House group
of companies whose addresses can be found at
global.penguinrandomhouse.com

Penguin
Random House
UK

First published in Great Britain by Young Arrow in 2021

www.penguin.co.uk

A CIP catalogue record for this book is available from the
British Library

ISBN 9781529120059

P......... in Great .... Grafica Veneta S.p.A.

The .... Penguin Random House
....
......

Penguin Random House is committed to a sus-
.... future for our business, our readers
.... from Forest
......

John Herzog is an award-winning illustrator. He also teaches illustration at Ringling College of Art & Design. John is a member of the National Cartoonists Society and SCBWI, and lives in Florida with his wife, two kids, and a menagerie of various animals. Please visit www.johnherzog.art to see more of his work.

SCAREDY CAT

A Word From SCAREDY CAT

Pay close attention.

Closer.

Even closer.

Oh, that's so much better. Except for your breath. Reminds me of a dog I met once.

Now listen to me. L—I—S—T—E—N. Oh, yes. I'm used to being listened to. I demand it. I insist on it. I will be listened to!!!

You've heard of Scaredy Cats, correct? Nod your head if you're listening. Now nod your head if I'm right. Aha, you *have* heard of Scaredy Cats.

Well, I'm a real Scaredy Cat, but, as you will see,

I'm not the one who is afraid. Oh, no. That should be you. Mee-OWWWWW!

There are others like me. Not nearly as talented, or fierce, or clever. But there are Scaredy Cats in your small town, your big city, your neighborhood, maybe even your backyard. We Scaredy Cats are everywhere. It's just that human beings can't see us. Only cats can see a Scaredy Cat.

Are you with me so far, dear hearts?

I am the Scaredy Cat on Strawberry Lane—a cul-de-sac (look it up) in the western suburbs of Fairview. The homes here are very lovely. Practically mansions. Why, there's even a gorgeous green golf course. Strawberry Lane runs right alongside the back nine. That's what golfers call the final holes on an eighteen-hole course. (You can look that up, too!)

Everything was going as it should. Fine and dandy, the cat's meow. But then a certain family moved to Strawberry Lane. That would be the Wilde family.

But why should I care about these Wildes?

I don't.

In fact, I couldn't care less about all human beans. They mean nothing to a Scaredy Cat as magnificent as I.

My complete focus was on the Wildes' two cats, whom they brought with them to my domain!

Poop, two and a half, a gray British shorthair. And yes, the vet gave her that name in honor of her nervous bowel syndrome. The name stuck. So did poop to the sides of her litter box. She's better now. But, well, let's just say I aim to make her bowels nervous again.

The other Wilde cat? Pasha, almost four, born in St. Petersburg. No, not St. Petersburg, Florida. St. Petersburg, *Russia*. Pasha is a white long-haired Persian cat. Speaks six languages. Once met Vladimir Putin, or so he claims. Repeatedly.

Now, this is important for our story. You must have noticed that cats are, shall we say, a teensy-weensy bit totally crazy, spooked-out, cat-eyed paranoid!

Always looking over their shoulders. Skittish. Often staring down long hallways at nothing. Frequently gazing out windows at...nothing. Jumping off couches and benches, and tables, and mantelpieces when they hear the slightest *poof* of a noise.

Well, Scaredy Cats are why they do that.

I am why they do that.

To be as clear as I can, I am a shadowy presence

that only cats can see. I'm not exactly a ghost, but that's a good way to think about me—especially if you don't think very well.

I'm scarier than any human ghost, though, because, as I'm sure you know, cats are far superior to humans in every way.

My job, my duty—nay, my calling—is to make sure that the cats in my realm act more cattish than any other cats on this planet or any other. My mission, should I choose to accept it, and I have, is to maintain the proper cat order, the catus quo, to resist any and all change to our cattiness or cattitude.

Cats are proud, cats are stubborn, cats are finicky, and I plan to keep it that way, especially in *my* domain!

And that is precisely the way life was on Strawberry Lane until Poop and Pasha arrived on my cul-de-sac. (Haven't you looked it up yet? I told you to look it up paragraphs ago!)

Here's what happened. And I should warn you—this is not a happy story. This, dear hearts, is a ghost story.

Chapter 1

That's a pretty good picture of me. I really am that gorgeous.

You should've seen my kitten pictures. Adorable.

Allow me to introduce myself. I'm Poop. Formerly of London. Currently residing in Fairview, USA. And yes, I used to have an, uh, issue. I'm all better now. Thanks for asking. Besides, I love my name. It makes human beans say, "Time to scoop Poop's poop."

Anyway, six months after moving from London to the United States, I could tell that things weren't really working out for me in my first home.

Don't get me wrong. The place was comfy. Plenty

of food, a nice fluffy bed, lots of toys (some filled with catnip), a jumbo-sized litter box, and fifteen different rooms for me to romp around in. There were also window shades with strings attached. Love me some string to tug.

But I liked to sleep in front of the TV. I couldn't help it. TVs are warm. The people inside them are often highly entertaining. So I'd just curl up in a ball and snooze, snuggled up against that cozy, toasty screen. I didn't know I was blocking the bottom part of the picture or that the bottom part of the picture was so earth-shatteringly important to the Man's enjoyment of sporting events.

"I can't see if the putt made it into the cup!" he'd shout. "The cat's butt's blocking half the green!"

When he said that, I rolled over—in classic belly rub position. No belly rub was forthcoming.

"Her belly's more bloated than her butt!" the Man growled at the Woman. "This lazy cat cost us four hundred pounds. Now she almost weighs that much!"

Pounds are what people in England—where I was born—use for money. I believe, if what I read in the business section of the newspaper I peed on this morning (the litter box was sooooo far away) is correct, four hundred British pounds equals about five hundred American dollars.

Why so much? Well, first of all, you saw my picture, right? I am *so* worth it.

Second, the Woman insisted that the Man purchase her a stunning, purebred, imported-from-jolly-old-England British shorthair cat with gray fur to match all the dove-gray furniture in the living room, no matter the cost. She found me online, paid to have me shipped over from England. She kept the name the London vet had given me. (I think she thought *poop* meant something else in jolly old England. You know, like *chips* meaning "French fries.")

Anyhow, that was then, this is now.

"I'm thinking of remodeling" is what the Woman said in reply to the Man when he so rudely complained about my butt and belly blocking his TV.

"What?" he growled.

"Gray is so last year. I want to do the whole house over in crisp blacks and whites." She flapped a magazine at the Man. "A black-and-white tuxedo cat would work much better with our new decor."

"Fine. That means this tubby tabby has to go."

"She's not a tabby, honey. She's a gray British shorthair. But yes. She should go. The sooner the better. The decorator is dropping by tomorrow and I don't want to insult her color scheme or delicate sensibilities..."

"Fine," snarled the Man. "It's worth five times five hundred dollars to have my TV back the way it's supposed to be!"

The Man grabbed me by the scruff of my neck and very unceremoniously, if you ask me, tossed me out the door into the backyard.

I remember it was a cold and drizzly night.

My paws plodded through puddles as I made my way to the garbage cans. What can I say? I was hungry. Emotional distress is a food trigger for me.

But as I approached the trash barrels set out near the curb, I heard a hiss.

Then two orange eyes started glowing in the darkness between the trash bins.

It scared me silly. I would've pooped my pants except cats don't wear pants, so I just pooped on the lawn.

The evil creature hissed again.

I took off running. Okay, I jogged. Fine, it was more of a waddle.

I headed to the nearest clump of trees. I was too terrified to pay attention to where I was going.

And that's how I ended up lost.

The next morning, however, I was found.

Not by my people.

Oh, no. I was hauled away by a burly fellow who worked for something called the Fairview Animal Care Center. It sounded lovely. A place where all they did was take care of animals. I was expecting an endless kibble buffet, dangly things on strings to chase, and constant belly rubs.

I was wrong.

It was a prison.

PASHA

Chapter 2

Zdravstvuyte vse! Ciao a tutti! Hallo zusammen!

Hello, everyone.

Okay, that's four languages. I could do more, but that would just bog down our story, wouldn't it?

As I'm certain you know from reading the caption under the illustration (always a wise thing to do), I am Pasha. Vladimir Putin gave me that name when he visited my home city. *Pasha* means "small" in Russian. Mr. Putin can be so cruel sometimes.

As I'm certain you can tell from the charming sketch, I am a BIG, gorgeous hunk of long-haired Persian masculinity. My fur? It is whiter than white rice thrown at a Siberian husky wedding in a blizzard.

Ah, my friends, my comrades, *mis amigos*—what a life I have led.

In my four years, I have experienced more than most cats experience in all nine of their lives.

Professor Heinrich von Schnitzel found me while he was visiting my home, St. Petersburg. The one in Russia, not Florida.

The learned professor, naturally, recognized a kindred spirit and keen intellect when he saw me scavenging for the finest scallop scraps and licking caviar tins behind La Marée, the famed Russian seafood restaurant at 34 Suvorovskiy Avenue.

The professor adopted me and filled out all the necessary papers and forms to have me shipped home with him to the United States. I still remember the first time I saw the Statue of Liberty. It was in the professor's den. He has a small bronze model of it that he uses as a paperweight.

I was the professor's only companion, except, of course, for his books. Oh, did he have books. They were stacked and piled everywhere. Sometimes, at night, he would read to me as I curled up and purred in his lap. I suppose it was his reading out loud to me that made me so superintelligent. So intellectually curious.

However, not too long ago, our nightly reading and purring sessions ended abruptly. So did almost everything in the house. Fortunately, one of the nice ladies in white who dropped by to take care of the professor ate tuna fish and saltines for lunch most days. She'd share some of her canned tuna with me. I also got most of the tuna juice.

Then came the *noctem horrendam*. That's Latin. I really don't count it as one of the languages I speak because, frankly, nobody really speaks Latin anymore. Pity, that. Anyway, the *noctem horrendam* means the "horrible night."

"He needs to go into an assisted living facility," I heard a very serious bald man say. He'd been listening to the professor's chest through a tube connected to earbuds. "He can't stay in his home any longer."

"We'll make the arrangements," said the sad woman I knew to be the professor's daughter. She dressed in tweed like he did. She never brought me a toy or a treat. Not even on Christmas or October 29, which, as I'm certain you know, is National Cat Day. And yes, gifts are expected.

"What about the cat?" asked my tuna-fish–loving

angel in white. "What about Pasha?"

"I can't take him," said the daughter. "Both my son and my daughter are deathly allergic to him."

Well, I wasn't so keen on *them*, either.

"And the assisted living facility doesn't allow pets," she added for good measure.

"Call the animal shelter," suggested the bald man. "With any luck, they should be able to find Pasha a new loving home."

Luck? We were turning my future and my fate over to luck? Human beans can be so...so...*human*.

I was too smart to believe in luck.

But I wasn't smart enough to escape from my new prison: the Fairview Animal Care Center.

I was put in a cage and put up for adoption.

Oh, did I mention? It was a kill shelter!

That meant if I wasn't adopted within a certain period of time, they would put me to sleep.

Permanently!

Chapter 3

On my third day locked inside a cage at the Fairview Animal Care Center, I was really starting to feel as if nobody cared for me, which was hard to believe since I'm so darn cute and cuddly.

Even if my name is Poop.

Oh, sure, they brought me chunks of rubbery food in a paper tray and periodically cleaned my litter box. But where was the love? Where was the admiration? I hadn't had a good belly rub in ages. Plus, all the other cats trapped in their cages were totally freaking me out. One was a real yowler. Another *meep*ed instead of meowing.

I started losing weight. I groomed myself so much I hocked up a huge hairball, which stayed in my cage drying out until the lady who cleans the kitty litter once a day saw it.

"Gross," she said.

But she didn't clean it up. She just crinkled her nose, scooped my litter, and went about her business. So I got to work, furiously pawing at my kitty litter until enough went flying backward to cover up the disgusting wad of partially digested hair.

"Do you mind?" said the cat in the cage next to mine. Apparently, I was back-kicking my litter so strenuously, I'd pelted him with a few pellets.

"Sorry about that," I said, batting my eyes.

"*De nada,*" he said. "It was nothing. *Nichevo.*"

My next-cage neighbor was a handsome and exotic guy. Long white hair. Some kind of accent. Either Russian or Spanish. Maybe German. I'm not good with accents.

"*Nichevo* is Russian for 'nothing,'" he graciously explained. "My name is Pasha, by the way. I speak six different languages."

"I just speak cat," I told him. "I'm curious…"

"Of course you are. You're a cat."

"Where are you from?"

"St. Petersburg."

"The one in Florida?"

"Hardly. Russia."

"Wow. No wonder you sound so, I don't know…"

"Exotic? Mysterious? Erudite?"

"Huh?"

"*Erudite* means 'having or showing great knowledge or learning.'" Pasha puffed up his chest with pride. "Not to brag, but I'm a genius."

"You're also extremely handsome."

"True."

"So, uh, if you're a handsome genius—how come you're locked in a cage just like me and all these other kitty cats?"

"Temporary setback. Minor inconvenience. I hope."

The way he said that last bit made me nervous. "You hope?"

"Yes…I'm sorry, I forgot to inquire as to your name."

"It's Poop."

There was a bit of a pause. "Seriously?"

"Yep. I've learned to live with it."

"Well, Poop, my hope is that someone comes along and adopts me. Pronto."

"I'm in no rush," I told him. "My last human beans weren't the best. They tossed me into the backyard without a collar, an ID tag, *or* a microchip. They threw me out like I was a sack of garbage, which, by the way, is what I had to eat for like one whole day. I was petrified. Afraid of my own shadow."

"Well," said Pasha, "as a very wise woman once said, 'The thing you fear most has no power. Your fear of it is what has the power.'"

"That was Oprah. Oprah Winfrey. She lives inside the TV."

"I am attempting to live by her words and not succumb to my fears," said Pasha, sounding extremely noble. "However, we only have four weeks."

"To do what?"

"To find new homes. Otherwise, they will put us to sleep."

"That's okay. I love to nap. Especially if I can find a good sunbeam."

"I don't think you understand the meaning of *to sleep*."

"Sure I do. It's what I do best."

"For goodness' sake, Poop! This is a kill shelter!"

My eyes bugged out. "What?"

"If we don't find a home in four weeks, they're going to kill us!"

And once again, it was a good thing I don't wear pants. Because I would've peed in them.

Instead I just peed on the soggy paper lining on the bottom of my cage.

PASHA

Chapter 4

I think I traumatized my next-cell neighbor.

Poor Poop. Her eyes were as wide as saucers filled with cream, which, by the way, despite what you've heard or seen in cartoons, cats should *not* lap up. Most of us are lactose intolerant. Hello, diarrhea. Good luck scooping *that* litter.

"We're gonna die!" Poop screeched. "We're all gonna die! This is a kill shelter! They kill cats here! And guess what? *We're all cats!!!*"

She screeched it so loudly, our fellow felines in the cage room went bonkers—whimpering, growling, hissing, and meowing miserably.

But then the doorknob rattled. The knob on the

door to the waiting room, not the other door that the workers used.

That meant someone was coming in, looking for a cat to adopt.

In an instant, all the caterwauling stopped. Cats gave their fur a quick lick and assumed their best *pick-me-pick-me* poses. I simply composed myself, settled into a portrait-worthy position, and let intelligence ooze out of my eyes.

One of the shelter volunteers led a family of four into the room.

The family seemed to be a loving if unconventional, freewheeling group. They were all laughing and giggling like they shared a secret joke that no

one outside their family could ever possibly understand. I liked them immediately.

The volunteer, on the other hand, was quite serious. She also had a clipboard.

"Just need to fill out this form, folks," she said.

"Okay," said the father of the brood, "we're the
Wildes."

"That makes me a Wilde child," said the shaggy-
haired boy. He seemed to be twelve-ish.

"And, if I may," said the volunteer, "what do you
do for a living, Mr. and Mrs. Wilde?"

"I make guitars and drums," said Mr. Wilde. "I fix
'em, too."

"Rock on!" shouted their daughter, a human
bean of about nine.

"That's Ash," said the father. "She's a little rocker.
Keyboard, guitar, and drums."

"I'm guessing your neighbors love that," com-
mented the volunteer.

"We don't know yet," said the mother. "We're
moving into a new home on Strawberry Lane. It's
closer to the Good Earth preschool."

"Not that any of us go to preschool," said the boy.
"Mom's a teacher there."

"You mean the *best* teacher there, Lance," added the father.

"Totally," said Lance.

"Rock oooooooon!" shrieked Ash.

This time, she pumped her fist in the air.

"I paint and sculpt," Lance said to the lady with the clipboard, gesturing that she might want to write that down. "I'm going to be like the next Michelangelo. Or da Vinci. Maybe even Banksy. He spray-painted a cat. On a wall. He didn't spray-paint on an actual cat..."

"And da Vinci did quite a study of cats," added the boy's mother.

That's when the father started singing, *"With two cats in the yard, life used to be so hard..."*

"We want two cats," said the mom.

"Well," said the volunteer, "that's wonderful. We have a lot to choose from..."

"We want those two!" said Ash. She'd struck a pose like a rock star pointing out at her adoring crowd with both hands.

Fortunately, she was pointing at Poop.

And me!

PASHA

Chapter 5

The next morning, Poop and I woke up in our new home on Strawberry Lane!

Actually, the home was new for the Wildes, too. They were busily unpacking boxes, putting things away in closets and cupboards, leaving all sorts of empty cardboard cartons and packing material behind.

"It's a kitty Disney World!" declared Poop.

"I agree!"

I took a delightful tumble into a box. Of all the cat toys ever invented, the cardboard carton is the best! For me, there's nothing quite as entertaining as an empty box, especially if there's crumpled packing

paper in it, too. I believe this is why cats in Canada and other countries celebrate Boxing Day.

"I feel so, so...*safe*!" gushed Poop from deep within an empty carton labeled KITCHEN STUFF.

We felines love a good enclosed space. In the wild (for instance, the alley behind an upscale Russian seafood restaurant), confined quarters like boxes allow us to both hide from our enemies and stalk our prey—such as the busboy who emptied those caviar tins into the dumpster.

I must say, the Wildes were living up to their name.

Ash, the girl, was using empty boxes of various sizes to improvise a very jazzy drum solo in her room. Lance was using his empty boxes to build a robot. Then a pyramid. Then a cave maze. All of his cardboard sculptures were very clever and creative. He also allowed me to play in them.

"That is so cool, Lance," said Mr. Wilde when he saw one of his son's box creations. "Can I crawl around in it?"

"Totally. But you better hurry. I'm having another inspiration. I'm going to flatten all the cardboard and make a ski slope down the staircase."

"Awesome!"

Mrs. Wilde was loading a box with toys the kids had brought to the new house but weren't really interested in anymore.

"I'll take these all to school with me. Toys need kids to play with them, otherwise their lives lose their purpose."

"True," said the wise nine-year-old Ash. "I've seen all the *Toy Story* movies."

The house was chaotic that day (as it would be most days), but the Wildes were having fun. With the task at hand. With each other.

That night, we all sat around the kitchen island

sharing Chinese food. Poop and I took turns sitting in various laps. Sampling pinches of the Kung Pao shrimp. Marking and bonding with our new family.

"Tomorrow's Saturday," announced Mr. Wilde. "I'll head over to the home improvement store. Get a pet door. Give these two a little freedom to be indoor-outdoor cats."

"They're microchipped, right?" said Mrs. Wilde.

"Yes. The shelter took care of that. If they get lost, a vet can scan their backs and know where their home is. Here. With us!"

And then the whole family held hands and started singing that "With two cats in the yard" song in four-part harmony. It was beauteous.

That night, as Poop and I snuggled down into our soft, blanket-lined box beds (new pet beds with built-in warmers were also on Mr. Wilde's Saturday morning shopping list), I let out a contented sigh.

"Poop, my new young friend, we have definitely landed in the gravy. As they say in my former home, Russia, 'We used to live and spill tears, now we live and build happiness.'"

"They say that? Really?"

"*Da*. It sounds way better in the original Russian,

but they say it when they're as happy as a clam. Although to be honest, I never understood why clams were so happy. So many of them end up in chowder…"

"Pasha?"

"Yes, Poop?"

"I'm afraid."

"Of what? These Wildes are the perfect human beans."

"I know. I rubbed all their legs. That's how much I love them already. But…the door!"

"I beg your pardon?"

"The pet door. It will open into the backyard!"

"So?"

"I've only gone outside in my carrier when my old human beans took me to the vet or the groomer or the claw clipper. And then…there was the night… when…I was…TOSSED OUTSIDE! Into the yard. I had to eat garbage. It didn't taste very good."

I had to chuckle a little. "Relax. The outdoors is marvelous. Fresh air. Lovely flowers. Birds."

"There're birds?"

"Everywhere. But only to look at. Not to attack."

"Of course."

"Don't worry, kiddo," I told her. "There's nothing to be afraid of outdoors. And I'll be there to protect you every step of the way!"

Of course, I said all that before we'd met the neighborhood Scaredy Cat.

Chapter 6

Sunday afternoon, after running around all day Saturday gathering supplies, Mr. Wilde, with the help of Lance and Ash, started running VERY LOUD power tools to install a flapping pet entrance in the kitchen door—the one that led out to the backyard.

Pasha was so excited as we perched on the kitchen island to observe the home improvement project. I had my paws over my ears.

"This is our Independence Day, Poop!" Pasha proudly proclaimed. "Once that door is installed, we shall be forever free! Indoor? Outdoor? The choice shall be ours!"

Me? I was still afraid of going outside. Plus, inside

was air-conditioned. I didn't think the outdoors was. Inside, it's a crisp and constant seventy-four degrees. Out there? It's whatever temperature the sun decides on that day.

"Hmm," said Mr. Wilde after Lance cut out a thick chunk of wood from the bottom panel. "Guess you should've used a level. That hole's a little lopsided."

"So?" said Lance, who, like his father and sister, was covered with sawdust. "Who says everything has to be perfectly square?"

"Only squares, man," said Ash, who, even though she was nine, sounded like a jazz hipster. I've seen and heard some of those inside the TV.

"You're right," said the father. "It has more personality this way!"

Mrs. Wilde joined the construction crew because, from what I'd learned in our short time with the family, these Wildes liked to do everything together. Mrs. Wilde screwed the pet door into place. Several of the screws made grinding, screeching noises that made me jump back and bump into a bowl.

"Relax," chuckled Pasha. "It's just a little noise. Nothing to be afraid of."

Ha! That's what he thought. Every single surprising noise ever made was enough to make me jumpy.

Car horns. Microwave *ding*s. Boots hitting the floor in the mudroom. Fortunately, I could always tell when Ash was about to bang her drums or snarl her guitar or pound her keyboard. She always announced it with some kind of rock-star–ish proclamation such as "Let's rock!" or "Cleveland, this is for you!"

After dinner (a delicious bowl of Fancy Feast Classic Paté, thank you for asking), the pet door was finally complete.

"Bravo!" said Pasha when the Wildes stepped back to admire their slightly tilted handiwork. "Freedom is ours, Poop. We can now come and go as we please. Ready to head outside and listen to the melodious chirping of the birds? Perhaps chase a butterfly flitting between flowers? Or simply savor the grassy scent of a newly mown lawn?"

"Um, no, thanks, Pasha. Maybe, you know, tomorrow." I stretched my whole body—from my splayed-open front paws up my spine to my curling tail. "I need a nap. Watching human beans work and sweat and churn up sawdust is sooooo exhausting."

"A quick game of chase in the backyard will revive you, my friend! Come on. Let us romp and relish our first day of indoor-outdoor activities!"

"Nopers. Just going to chillax for a few hours.

Curl up in front of a warm TV and snoozle."

"Poop?"

"Yes, Pasha?"

"Fear is a prison. Its bars are strong. And only you have the key to unlock the cage door you've welded for yourself."

"Oh. Is that something else they say in Russia?" I replied cattily. "Go ahead. Run around outside. Get burrs and nettles and dead leaves in that long white fur of yours. Come back looking like something the cat dragged in. Me? I'm taking a nap. And when I'm done napping, I'm gonna eat a snack. And when I'm done snacking, I'm gonna take another nap. Napping is what I do! And guess what, Pasha? I'm really, really good at it!"

PASHA

Chapter 7

"I'm sorry if you thought I was being harsh, Poop," I told my new best friend late Sunday night when it was time for her to wake up from her third nap and start roaming around the house.

I roamed with her.

"That's okay, Pasha," she said. "I think I was hangry. You know—I was so hungry I got angry. That's what *hangry* means."

"But you had that whole bowl of Fancy Feast."

"And your point is?"

Monday, even though there was a terrible rain shower that Poop thought should've prompted the authorities to close down the out-of-doors, the

Wildes grabbed their umbrellas and rain slickers and set off to their other worlds. Mr. Wilde to the woodshop where he crafted his musical instruments. Mrs. Wilde to her job at the Good Earth preschool. Lance and Ash to school.

"We have the whole house to ourselves!" said Poop as she warmed up her paws on the scratching post the Wildes had purchased for us over the weekend.

"And, if I may," I reminded her, "we will also have the whole backyard—once the rain ceases and the sun has dried up the more pernicious puddles."

"I'm not so sure I want to visit the backyard, Pasha."

"Not right now, of course. It's a monsoon out there. A torrential downpour, as it were. But later, when the storm passes, it can't be missed. Why, in my preliminary explorations, I discovered a delightful birdbath where many birds were splashing about."

"And you watched them? Taking a bath?"

"Oh, yes."

"That's kind of creepy, Pasha. Creepy."

Later that afternoon, after her fourth nap, Poop led me into the TV room.

"Since it's still raining out, I thought you might

enjoy watching one of my favorite shows. Lance tuned it to the YouTube cat channel." She nodded up at the TV screen. It showed a video of a group of brightly colored birds pecking seeds off a stump.

"Poop? Honestly. Why would we watch a TV channel about birds when, once this storm passes, we'll have—"

I did not get to complete that thought.

Thunder boomed. Rain blew sideways and splattered against all the windows. The lights in the house flickered and, just like that, we had a visitor. A shadowy cat with glowing orange eyes had just, somehow, appeared. Did it sneak in through our pet door? Doubtful. First, it wasn't in the least bit wet and it was storming outside. Second, I don't think its turban would've fit.

That's right, this mean-looking, malevolent monster of a cat was wearing a silk fortune-teller turban clasped in the front with a sparkling emerald brooch. He also wore a very shiny red silk robe that wafted behind him in slow motion—without any wind!

"What be your namessss?" he hissed.

Every hair on Poop's back sprang up. She was terrified. Then she piddled. On the carpet. It made that *tickety-tickety-tick-tick* noise.

"I sssaid, what be your namesss?"

"Seriously?" I told it. "You're going full pirate on us?"

"Sssilence, you paltry house pet."

"Paltry? House pet? I'll have you know I am an international traveler. I used to live in St. Petersburg. And not the one in Florida."

"I care not," he said with a sinister sneer. "For I am your friendly neighborhood Scaredy Cat. Although you can forget the 'friendly' bit. I haven't done 'friendly' in agesss. You two are hereby and forthwith sssummoned to a meeting of all the cats in my Strawberry Lane domain. This evening. Midnight. Be there."

"Oh, of course," I said. "Not!"

His eyes flared bright orange. Owl ears of angry hair sprang up on both sides of his turban.

"You would dare defy me?"

"I wouldn't," peeped Poop.

"We don't believe in Scaredy Cats," I said as boldly as I could, what with the thunder booming and lightning flashing. "Who would?"

"I might," squeaked Poop.

"No, you wouldn't," I told her. "Scaredy Cats are simply myths and legends. Any cat could have their people buy them a Halloween costume at Petco and then use it to go around the neighborhood terrorizing civilized cats who don't believe in such foolishness."

"You insignificant infidel! Believe in me, Pasha!"

Okay. That kind of got me.

"How do you know my name? I never told you..."

"You are on my street now, Pasha. I know everything about every cat on Strawberry Lane. You, too, Poop. Oh, yes. I know your name, too. And where it came from." He waved a paw in front of his nose. "Both of you must be at the meeting tonight at midnight or you will suffer the conssssequencessss!"

He went up on his haunches and unfurled his front claws.

"Mee-ooooowwwww!"

When he did that, I heard another *tickety-tickety-tick-tick.*

Poop had peed on the rug. Again.

Chapter 8

I couldn't believe that Pasha was back-talking a Scaredy Cat.

He might not have thought Scaredy Cats were real, but I sure did. Remember those glowing orange eyes I saw between the garbage cans outside my old home? Hello! That was probably a Scaredy Cat. No, that was *definitely* a Scaredy Cat. Or maybe a raccoon. It could've been a raccoon, which, by the way, would also terrify me.

"You have irritated me, Pasha," proclaimed the Scaredy Cat. "And, by your very presence with this ungrateful Russian street urchin, you have also offended me, Poop!"

Meowzers. He could really make my name sound stinky. I think I would've peed the carpet again but my bladder was running on empty.

"Prepare ye to ssssuffer the conssssse-quenccccessssss!"

That last sentence was a lawn sprinkler of hiss spittle.

Then, because, IMHO, this wild-eyed fur face was definitely a Scaredy Cat, the maniac darted into the kitchen, where he committed all sorts of mayhem and mischief. The kind of stuff that could get a cat tossed to the curb by the scruff of her neck again.

He tipped over the litter box, sending pellets and wet clods skittering and scattering across the tile floor.

"Stop that," said Pasha, as if words could slow down the demon who was now running along the countertops knocking over everything he encoun-tered, including an unspooling roll of paper towels and a dangling clump of bananas. The bananas hit the floor with a very wet *SQUISH!*

Then it was time for him to shred the morning newspaper and tip over our brand-new sculpted pottery water bowls. They were so cute, too. Next

Scaredy Cat gobbled down all our kibble. It was supposed to last Pasha and me all day!

"Don't fret, Poop," he said with a malicious smile. "There's more kibble where that came from."

It was as if the crazed creature could read my mind. Maybe that's why he wore a turban. He was one of those mind readers I'd seen inside the TV.

With one mighty swat of his meaty paw, Scaredy Cat bopped open one of the lower cabinets to expose the twenty-five-pound bag of cat food our human beans had purchased for us. He snapped out his claws. I swear they sprang up one at a time with sharp metallic clicks. Scaredy Cat swiped those razor-sharp hooks against the bottom of the feed sack. At least twenty pounds of slippery brown pellets cascaded out of the gash and spread across the floor, where they mingled with the mashed bananas.

Then, and this was impressive, he used his left paw to open the refrigerator with a single swat.

"Oh, my, such a fine collection of explode-able food items," he purred with glee. Actually, his purr sounded more like a rumbling rasp from a wheezing motor scooter.

Next thing I knew, a dozen eggs were splattered on the kitchen floor. Then tomatoes. And button mushrooms. And a jar of pickle relish. And a jar of mayonnaise. It was like the thing wanted to whip up an omelet with a side order of tartar sauce.

When he pulled himself up onto the top shelf of the fridge, he spun his head around horror movie style—a full 180 degrees—and glared down at Pasha and me.

"Shall I slice open the orange juice next, or have you two learned your lessssson?"

I was about to answer with an "Uh, yeah. Duh." But there was a noise outside. The hiss of a bus air-braking to a stop.

I heard a door swing open and children laughing. School was done for the day. Next came the sound of rubber-booted feet splashing in puddles near the curb.

It was after three. Lance and Ash were home!

"All right, *moy droog, mi amigo,* my friend," said Pasha, arching his back so high it looked like a suspension bridge. "You need to leave here. You need to leave here immediately. Our human beans are home."

"I shall be on my way, then. I could care less about human beans. It's you two who are my responsibility. I shall see you both this evening. At the mandatory meeting. Be there at midnight or beware my wrath!"

"We don't want your wrath," I assured the creepy thing, nodding toward the mess in the kitchen. "We've had enough wrath to last us nine lives."

"This? Why, this is but a mere preview of what I might do if provoked. And whatever you do, do not follow me. Any cat that follows me shall never return. Mee-OWWWWW!"

There was one more thunderclap, one more flash of lightning, and Scaredy Cat was—*POOF!*—gone.

"Why on earth would we want to follow you?" grumbled Pasha. "Mee-OWWWWW! right back at you, Creepy Claws!"

PASHA

Chapter 9

"Um, you guys?" said Lance as he and Ash came into the kitchen for an after-school snack.

He was talking to Poop and me, of course.

"What the heck happened in here?"

"Did you let the storm in through the back door?" added Ash.

I turned up my cuteness quotient by tilting my head slightly to the left and widening my eyes. As a street kitten, I had found that cuteness worked on the fishmongers back home in St. Petersburg. I nudged Poop, whose eyes were wide with horrified fear. She needed to switch into cute mode, pronto.

"I guess you two aren't used to living in a house,"

said Lance kindly. "Just those cramped cages at the animal shelter."

"Yeah," said Ash. "If I'd been cooped up my whole life, I'd go a little wild my first day alone, too."

"You go wild all the time," joked her big brother.

"Don't blame me, bro. Blame the music. Where the beat leads, I must follow."

Lance nodded. He was an artiste, too. He understood.

I wanted to say, *I beg your pardon, young man and young lady, but I was domesticated in the home of an eminent and learned professor for three full years.* But the human bean language is one I have yet to master.

"Come on, Ash," said Lance. "Let's clean this mess up before Mom gets home."

"Good idea. She'll be here in like twenty minutes."

Lance looked at me. "Is it just the kitchen or did you two trash the rest of the house, too?"

I mewled out an apologetic meow, which I hoped the boy understood to mean "Just the kitchen."

He nodded. Who needed language? We were communicating!

Poop, on the other hand, was still sitting there frozen. Staring off into space.

"Pssst! Poop?" I whispered. "We could use a little grateful cuteness from you. The children are protecting us. They're tidying up the Scaredy Cat's mess."

"Aha!" Poop whispered back. "You admit that thing was a Scaredy Cat!"

"I am only using the name it gave itself. I respect its choice to call itself whatever it chooses."

"It's a Scaredy Cat! A Scaredy Cat, Scaredy Cat, Scaredy Cat!"

She yowled it so loudly, Lance and Ash quit sweeping up kibble and wiping up egg yolks.

"You okay, Poop?" asked Ash.

"She probably heard Mom and Dad talking last night," said Lance. "The whole two-week trial thing."

"We wouldn't really send them back, would we?" asked Ash.

Lance shrugged. "I dunno. If they keep making a mess like this, we might have to. They might be too wild to live with the rest of us Wildes!"

When Lance said that, both he and Ash had a good laugh.

"Impossible, bro."

"Yeah. But Mom and Dad both said it. Plus, Dad has those allergies."

"He'll get over them," said Ash. "With time, he'll

build up an immunity to Pasha and Poop's dander. I know he will. And there're all sorts of allergy pills..."

"It's true," Poop whispered to me. "People inside the TV talk about allergy pills all the time. Maybe Mr. Wilde can ask his doctor if one of those medications is right for him. The TV is always telling people to ask their doctors whether medicines are right for them."

The kids finished cleaning up the mess. I rubbed myself against their pants, weaving in and out between their legs to express my gratitude. Poop followed right behind me and did the same.

Lance and Ash both grabbed a piece of fruit and headed upstairs to do their homework.

"That was close," I said with a sigh.

Poop's eyes bugged out in fear again. "Do you really think we're here on a two-week trial? Do you think Mr. and Mrs. Wilde will send us back to that animal-care center?"

Outside, the rain had finally stopped. Clouds were parting. A shaft of late-afternoon sunlight streamed through the window over the sink.

"No, Poop," I said sunnily. "This, my friend, is to be our forever home!"

Just then, Scaredy Cat reappeared in the arched

doorway that leads from the kitchen into the dining room. This time he was wearing a pointed, jewel-encrusted Mongolian hat with a fluffy pom-pom at its tip. He had also slipped into a green silk robe embroidered with Chinese dragons. Leather sword holsters crisscrossed his chest.

"Apologiesssss," he hissed. "I forgot to tell you where the meeting is this evening. Number Nine Strawberry Lane. The empty house two doors up the block. It is, as they say, for ssssale. Look for the sign in the front lawn. Be there at the stroke of midnight. Or else."

"Or else what?" I snapped back.

"Or else this will keep happening!"

And then, in a blur of silk and fur and flying claws, the monster in the Genghis Khan costume tore through the kitchen like a whirling cyclone, making another mess where Lance and Ash had just tidied up.

Chapter 10

"We'll be there!" I shrieked.

"No, we won't!" cried Pasha.

"Will, too!"

"Won't!"

"Will!"

"Courage must rise, Poop, in the face of tyranny!"

"No, it mustn't!"

"Ssssilence," hissed Scaredy Cat.

Then he marched right up to Pasha's face, his breath stinking of tuna fish that'd been rotting in the trash since a week ago Tuesday. I could smell it and I was halfway across the room, hiding behind the bruised clump of bananas the evil thing had flung back down to the floor.

"You would be wise to listen to your pretty little friend, Pasha. Midnight. Number Nine. Strawberry Lane. You will do as I command. Or you will most certainly fail your two-week trial."

Pasha bristled. "How on earth could you know about that?"

"I told you: this is my cul-de-sac."

"Cul-de-sac?" I said.

"Look it up! Suffice it to say, on Strawberry Lane, I know everything."

And with a *POOF!*—he vanished. He did that a lot.

I was so frightened I had to pant a little, which is something we cats only do in extreme heat or high-stress situations.

"I need a moment," I told Pasha, fanning my face with a paw.

But I didn't get my moment. Mrs. Wilde came through the back door with a stack of pizza boxes.

"Oh my goodness," she said when she saw the mess in the kitchen. "Lance? Ash?"

The kids thudded down the steps from their rooms and came into the kitchen.

"Again?" said Lance, shaking his head and look-ing at the mess, then looking at us.

"Dudes?" said Ash, crouching down to pat me on the head and rub my ears. I like having my ears rubbed. "Seriously. You two can't keep making a mess."

"They did this before?" said Mrs. Wilde.

"Sort of," said Lance, doing his best to cover for us. "I mean, they'd tipped over their water bowl."

"Just a little," added Ash.

I liked these Wilde children. And I think they REALLY liked me. Probably Pasha, too. They were protecting us from the doom of the two-week trial.

"So...," said Mr. Wilde, coming in from the living room, toting a pair of brightly colored reusable shop-ping bags. "What happened here?"

"We had a thunderstorm of our own," said Mrs. Wilde with a laugh. "Indoors."

Lance had already started wiping up the mashed guacamole on the floor. Ash was scooping up kibble. "We should probably get a plastic bin for their food," she suggested. "The bottoms on these bags keep rip-ping open..."

"Good idea," said Mrs. Wilde, grabbing a broom and a dustpan.

Mr. Wilde took a nasal sprayer out of one of his

shopping bags and gave his nostrils a double squirt of allergy medicine.

Yes. It was true. The man was allergic to Pasha and me! No way were we going to pass our two-week test. We were going back behind bars at the cat prison!

"Poop?" said Mrs. Wilde, gently sweeping with her broom. "Pasha? We all have to respect each other's space, okay? We have to help keep our classroom, I mean kitchen, clean. In this house, we play safely. We look out for each other. We use our indoor voices."

"She speaks wisdom, my feline friends," said Mr. Wilde, who was also helping clean up the mess Scaredy Cat had left behind (again). "Let's all stay mellow and keep on keepin' on." Then he started singing a song. *"Get back, honky cat!"*

Ash picked up the beat with a wooden spoon on the bottom of a plastic bowl. Mrs. Wilde and Lance joined in the singing while they swept and scrubbed and swished up spills with paper towels. Some human beans whistle while they work. The Wildes sang. In no time, the kitchen was tidy again. It was almost as if Scaredy Cat had never been there.

Almost.

PASHA

Chapter 11

Later that evening, as I was snoozing in my new plug-in electric-warmer bed, I was quite surprised when Poop came over and started making biscuits on my back.

You know, doing that double-paw kneading thing as if I were a wad of freshly rolled-out dough.

"Pasha?" she whispered. "Are you awake?"

"I am now."

"It's eleven thirty. We need to go to that meeting."

"What meeting?"

Poop gave me an exasperated exhale. "The one that Scaredy Cat summoned us to. Nine Strawberry Lane. We have to go there or else!"

"Or else what?" I said with a yawn.

"Something terrible. And horrible. And not much fun."

"But, Poop," I said with a sly grin, "to attend this meeting we must first venture outside."

"I know that."

"We'll have to use the pet door."

"I know."

"And traipse across the mysterious backyard."

"I know!!!" Poop screeched as quietly as she could. "It's worth the risk, Pasha. We're living in that monster's cul-de-sac."

"Did you look that up? *Cul-de-sac*?"

"No. But it can't mean anything good."

"Fine. We'll go. But only to observe. I will not swear blind allegiance and fidelity to any cat except myself and, perhaps, you, Poop. For you are my friend."

Poop gasped. "Is that what you think that thing wants us to do? To pledge allegiance to him? Does he think he's a flag?"

I nodded. "Such is my suspicion. My former human bean, the professor, often read to me about history's tyrants. Cruel and oppressive bullies who used fear tactics to keep a quivering, terrified population in line. I suspect our Scaredy Cat is the reigning tyrant of this particular cul-de-sac, which, by the way, means this is not a through street. There's no exit. It dead-ends in a circle, only allowing you to go back out the way you came in."

"You're smart."

"It's what I do, Poop. It's what I do."

"And you really think Scaredy Cat is trying to scare us into submission?"

I nodded again.

"Well," said Poop, "he's doing a pretty darn good job. I'm so afraid, I lost a whisker and a clump of fur off my butt."

"We have nothing to fear, Poop, but fear itself."

"And Scaredy Cat. We have that orange-eyed monster to fear, too."

"Fine. Let's go see what the monster has to say."

PASHA

Chapter 12

I led the way through the flapping pet door.

Poop was right on my tail. Literally.

"Poop?"

"Yes, Pasha?"

"Dogs sniff each other's butts. Not cats."

"Right. Sorry."

We scurried through the dewy grass of the backyard and around the side of the house until we hit the paved driveway. It took us to the sidewalk. Somewhere, an owl hooted.

"Meowzers!" screeched Poop. "What was that?"

"An owl hooting. Somewhere."

"The outdoors at night is even scarier than the daytime!"

"Shhh," I said, nudging Poop behind a shrub where we could crouch down and spy on Number Nine Strawberry Lane. "There's the For Sale sign. That must be Number Nine Strawberry Lane."

"You can read?"

"Of course. Plus, it's the only yard on the block with a sign planted in its lawn. And look at that line of cats streaming up the porch steps to the front door, which someone has propped slightly open. Ipso facto, this is where the meeting is being held."

"Look!" said Poop. "Silhouettes on the shades. More cats. Dozens. They must be having their meeting in that front room."

"Then we'll sneak in through the back."

"But the meeting is in the front!" whined Poop. "Everybody else is using the front door. It's closer, too. We wouldn't have to scamper so much. Scampering makes me hungry. I should've grabbed a snack before we left..."

"We're not everybody else and we're not going to the meeting. We're here to do research. To see if Scaredy Cat is a tyrant. To see if all the other cats on this street follow him with blind obedience. Follow me, Poop."

"Oh, so now you want to be the tyrant? A leader with followers?"

"No. I simply mean prowl where I prowl. Come after me."

We cats, as you might've heard, are extremely cunning and clever. Want to keep us out of something or some place? Good luck. We'll figure out a way in.

And so we did.

Around back, we discovered a bathroom window that someone had left propped open an inch or two—possibly to air out any unsavory odors.

With a quick high hop and a short belly scoot (which Poop mimicked in precise detail), we were soon inside the empty house.

I motioned for Poop to follow me up a hallway toward the living room, where I could see a wall filled with cat shadows. The shadows flickered and danced, as if someone had lit a fire in the fireplace and the neighborhood cats had all gathered around it.

"Cats of my cul-de-sac!" boomed a voice I

immediately recognized as that of Scaredy Cat. "This meeting is hereby called to order. All rise. Place your paws over your heart and recite the pledge!"

I'm sorry. When I heard that, I had to giggle. Inwardly, of course. One doesn't giggle out loud when doing surveillance work. But a pledge? That was rich.

The cats—at least two, maybe three dozen—rose in unison and droned these words:

I pledge allegiance to the almighty Scaredy Cat of Strawberry Lane and I do solemnly swear that I shall obey every command, decree, mandate, or demand my Scaredy Cat might make of me, day or night.

I was inwardly giggling so hard my whole body was shaking.

Poop looked torn. Between laughing and crying.

This was so ridiculous! But then the cats wound up for their big finish.

If I should fail my Scaredy Cat in any way at all, may I be banished to the wild and the woods. Or worse.

Chapter 13

Worse? What could be worse than banishment? I wondered.

Pasha motioned for me to follow him into an air duct.

I gave him my best *Are you nuts? I just bathed myself!* glare. Air ducts are filled with lint. And dust. And dusty lint.

He insisted. He pried open a vent covering with his claws and we scooted into a boxy sheet metal shaft that was pretty simple to scale because there were these crimped edges and screwheads we could clamp on to. In no time, we were in the ceiling looking down at the scene through a grate.

Scaredy Cat stood in front of a roaring fire. I think it was a gas fireplace where all you have to do is click the remote and the fake wood made out of concrete blazes away. My first human beans had one of those and I liked to bop the On switch with my paw—especially around the holidays. Very festive. Totally set the mood.

Anyway, Scaredy Cat was dressed in a new outfit. This one was very military-ish. Like he was a general with a hat and shoulder boards and a bunch of medals and ribbons pinned to his chest, which, if you ask me, was pretty dumb. Who wants to pin stuff to their fur? Maybe he used Velcro.

Thirty-three cats—all breeds, shapes, and sizes—were sitting at attention in three rings of semicircles, mesmerized by the evil monster's words. Scaredy Cat was perched on the top of a tall-backed chair, looking down on the adoring crowd. When he said something, they nodded in unison as if they were all feline bobblehead dolls. When he preened, they applauded. When he screamed something awful, they chanted it back. I've never seen so many yes-cats gathered together in one place in my life.

"Notice how Scaredy Cat has positioned himself above all the others?" whispered Pasha. "He wants

all of his subjects to know, in no uncertain terms, that he is the Top Cat!"

We pressed our ears to the ceiling grate to hear what Scaredy Cat was saying to whip up the neighborhood cats.

"You must always act the way I tell you to act!" Scaredy Cat shouted.

"We will, master," the rally crowd shouted back. "We will!"

"You must practice your looks of disdain!"

"We will do our due disdain duty!"

"You must turn up your nose at your food until the human beans race back and forth to the pet supply store to find a high-priced gourmet food you might like. And when you have eaten that food for five days, you must once again turn up your nose and send your human beans racing back to the pet store to find something more to your liking."

"We will remain finicky at all times!" the cats chanted.

"If your human beans call for you?"

"We will ignore them! We are not dogs!"

"When the lady of the house scolds you, what do you think in reply?"

"You are not my real mom!"

"If they don't scoop your litter swiftly enough?"

"Poop outside the box!"

"If your human beans attempt to sleep in?"

"We will knock everything off the night table until they feed us!"

"If they buy you an expensive toy?"

"We shall ignore it and play with the bag it came in."

"If they give you a scratching post?"

"We will continue to claw the closest chair."

"You have learned well, my minions," said Scaredy Cat, pleased with his power over his subjects.

"What a bunch of paw-licking sycophants," muttered Pasha.

That confused me a little. "I thought they were cats, not sick elephants..."

"A sycophant, Poop, is a toady, a brown-noser, a lickspittle, a flunky, a lackey, and a stooge—all rolled up into one disgusting hairball. Do you want to be like those cats down there? Going along to get along? Never playing or having fun? Never bonding with your human beans?"

"Not really," I whispered back. "They look like zombies. I'd rather look like a movie star, which many people already say I do. They tell me I could do cat food commercials. I'd like that. You get to eat in a cat food commercial."

"Want to show this Scaredy Cat once and for all that we're not afraid of him? That we refuse to fall in line?"

"No. Not really."

"Fine. Then go downstairs and join the mewling mob."

"Wait. What're *you* going to do?"

"Something daring, something bold, something wild."

"I like the Wildes," I said, because Pasha had used the word *wild* and my mind flits around like that. "The kids stood up for us. They cleaned up our mess. Twice."

"Then let's fight to live the life we want. Not the one Scaredy Cat wants to dictate to us."

I thought about that.

"Will it be scary?"

"Maybe," said Pasha. "But it should also be fun."

"Then let's do it!"

Chapter 14

"Follow me," I told Poop. "I noticed something when we were sneaking in."

"What?" she asked as we crawled down the air shaft. "That big porcelain water bowl in the bathroom? We have three of those back at the Wildes' house."

"No. In the hallway outside. On the wall. My professor had one. It's the control panel for this home's burglar alarm system!"

"Why didn't all those cats in the living room trigger it?" asked Poop.

"I suspect Scaredy Cat somehow disabled the motion sensors."

"He probably used magic."

"Poop? Scaredy Cat is not a magical creature. He is simply a bully cat."

"He seems kind of spooky. Like a magician. And he was wearing a turban that first time we met him and—"

"He is a cat," I insisted. "That is all. A cat we can scare off, just like any other."

We crawled out of the duct and crept back up the hall.

"There it is," I said, nodding up at the glowing panel.

"That's a lot of buttons," said Poop. "Which one triggers the alarm?"

"I have no idea," I confessed. "So I will simply have to swat them all."

Fortunately, I am an expert, dare I say Olympic-caliber, springer-upper. I can do the floor to the top of the refrigerator easily. So I leapt up and bopped a bunch of buttons. I leapt up again and slapped a few more. On the third jump, I hit the right combination. Alarm bells started ringing. A red light started swirling. A computerized voice droned, "Intruder alert. Intruder alert."

A thundering herd of terrified cats scrambled for the nearest exit.

"Come back here!" we heard Scaredy Cat bellow.

But that's the problem with ruling through fear. Your subjects aren't just afraid of you. They're afraid of everything.

"That was fun, Pasha," said Poop after we'd crawled out the bathroom window and started scurrying home.

"Yes," I said with a laugh. "It was a hoot."

We scooted through our pet door, nibbled a few crunchies out of our respective bowls, and hit our heated cat beds.

"Thanks, Pasha."

"You're welcome, Poop."

Then we both drifted off to sleep with grins on our faces that would've made the Cheshire Cat proud!

PASHA

Chapter 15

The next morning, after the Wildes had gone off to their assorted schools and workplaces, Poop surprised me.

"Let's go outdoors again!" she said.

"Are you serious?"

"Yeppers. Last night was so much…"

I think she was going to say "fun," but she didn't.

Because Scaredy Cat was back in our kitchen. Standing right in front of the back door. He was wearing his turban and cape again. His eyes were glowing bright orange. He was not a happy camper.

"Hello, Poop. Hello, Pasha. We misssssed you at the meeting."

"Was that last night?" I said with a smirk. "Golly, I had it on my calendar for tonight…"

Scaredy Cat bristled. "Oh, you are such a clever, clever kitty, aren't you, Pasha? Do you, for one instant, think with that little kumquat of a brain you have tucked inside your thick skull, that I don't know what you two did last night?"

"Technically," I said, "we did it very early this morning…"

"That's true," said Poop. "It *was* after midnight…"

"Sssilence, heretics! This is my cul-de-sac. I know everything that happens on Strawberry Lane. I see all. I smell all. I hear all. And—I saw you hopping up and down in the hallway, pawing at those alarm buttons."

"B-b-but," stammered Poop, "w-w-we didn't see you."

"Because I didn't want you to, foolish little girl. Do you doubt my powers?"

He shot his orange eyes to the left and stared intently at Mrs. Wilde's teakettle (she likes the herbal stuff). In seconds, it started steaming and whistling.

"Oh, my," chortled Scaredy Cat. "How'd that happen? Magic? Sorcery? Maybe a bit of both?"

He flicked his eyelids shut for a second, giving

the stove top the scariest slow-motion blink I've ever seen. The teakettle quit rattling and spewing steam. "Imagine what might happen if I decided to do that to you, Poop. Wouldn't that just make your blood boil? Mee-OWWWW!"

I heard a *tinkle-tinkle-tink-tink.*

This time Poop peed on the tile floor.

"You two *will* fall in line," declared Scaredy Cat. "You *will* obey me!"

"And if we don't?" I asked, sounding about half as defiant as I had a few minutes earlier. (I hate to admit it, but that teakettle trick was pretty impressive.)

"If you don't? My, my, my, what a foolish question, Pasha. Is that what the learned professor taught you? To ask dumb and insipid questions?"

"How do you know about—"

"How many times must I tell you, you ignorant alley cat? I KNOW EVERYTHING about every cat on Strawberry Lane. And those that have dared to challenge me? Oh, my. Things don't end well for them. Oh, no, not at all. In fact, they typically end up stranded in the woods. Starving. Hiding from the various predators who lurk there in the darkness. They revert to what they once were. They become

feral savages. Untamed. Uncivilized. Undomesti-
cated. Unloved! Cross me one more time, and that is
what will happen to you! You will be shunned and
then you will be *cast out*!"

Chapter 16

I needed to scour myself with a good tongue bath.

Well, at least my hind legs. They were all kinds of wet from where Scaredy Cat scared the peeweezus out of me.

The thing gave a maniacal meow, raised his cape like a vampire I'd seen on TV, and then—*POOF!* He disappeared in a cloud of orange smoke. The crazy cat was quite the showman.

It was just me and Pasha and my piddle puddle in the kitchen again.

"Well," said Pasha, puffing up his chest (and deflating his tail, which had billowed up into full Halloween cat/electrocuted mode to make him look more menacing). "This is a major turning point in our lives."

"It is?"

"Indeed. We are presented with a choice, Poop."

"Is one of the choices 'eat a snack'? Like I said, I'm an emotional eater..."

"No, Poop. This is a much grander decision. Perhaps the most important decision either one of us will ever make."

I gulped a little when he said that.

Pasha sat proudly on the floor, his spine straight, his tail curled confidently in front of his paws. "We can stay indoors, trembling in fear, following all of Scaredy Cat's rules."

"Or?" I asked, because I really liked the Wildes. I didn't want to be aloof and ignore them the way Scaredy Cat told all those cats at his meeting we were supposed to. Where's the fun in that? "What's our other option, Pasha?"

"We can embrace our newfound freedom." He nodded toward the pet door. "We can rally the neighborhood and encourage all the other cats in this cul-de-sac to join us in the quest for life, liberty, and the pursuit of purrs! Remember this, Poop—Scaredy Cat is but one angry and crazed beast."

"With fancy costumes," I added. "And some pretty neat magic tricks."

"True," said Pasha. "But there will always be more of us than there are of him. If we unite, if we rise up in resistance to his ridiculous rules, we can live the lives we were meant to live. Free of fear. Free of want. Free of laughable midnight meetings, a time when we'd much rather be prowling around our own homes hunting bottle caps and shooting them across the floor like skittle pool pucks."

"Aren't you afraid of what he might do to us?"

Pasha shook his head. "No, *mi amiga*. I am more afraid of what will become of me if I do nothing. As a wise man named Benjamin Franklin—who, by the way, had a pet angora cat—once said: 'Those who would give up essential Liberty to purchase a little temporary Safety, deserve neither Liberty nor Safety!'"

"He was a cat person?" I asked.

"Indeed so."

"Then he has to be smart. That does it. I'm with you, Pasha. Let's go rally the cul-de-sac. Give me freedom or give me a bath in the sink. It's time we stood up to Scaredy Cat!"

PASHA

Chapter 17

After fortifying ourselves at our cat bowls, chomping down on an exquisite and elegant mound of mashed and mushy meat, I led the way out the pet door.

Poop followed.

"I suggest we work the cul-de-sac logically," I announced. "We'll proceed in a clockwise manner."

"Okay," said Poop. "What does *clockwise* mean?"

"That we move in the same direction as a clock's hands. From here to the right and then looping back again on the far side of the street once we hit the end of Strawberry Lane."

"Oh. Okay. But what's that have to do with

a clock? All the ones I've ever seen have glowing numbers, not hands."

I sighed. "Yes. Such is the dreariness of the digital age. Come along, Poop. Keep your eyes alert and your ears up. We go in search of brother and sister cats."

"There!" squeaked Poop. "Preening in the front window. That was a cat."

"Indeed. A pampered Persian, if my eyes do not deceive me. Quickly, Poop. Let's scurry around to the back door."

"Why not the front?"

"Nobody puts flapping pet access panels in their *front* doors, Poop. It's against all the human bean rules."

"Oh. I did not know that."

"Stick with me, *ma jeune amie*. My time living with the learned professor taught me much!"

We scampered around to the back of the house and, much to my surprise, discovered there was no pet door. Just one made out of a screen mesh. Fortunately, since it was a breezy day, the kitchen door behind it was propped open.

"Excuse me?" I cried out. "Fellow feline? Might we have a moment of your time? Yoo-hoo?"

"Anybody home?!?" shrieked Poop. "We're here at the back door. The one behind the kitchen."

A massive ball of white fur with a turned-up snout and green eyes ambled around the kitchen island. It yawned when it saw us on the other side of the screen door. The cat was wearing a shimmering, shiny necklace.

"Sorry," it said. "I can't really come to the door right now. I am about to enjoy my midmorning snack. I do hope it will tide me over to my late-morning snack. Then I will probably poop. Then it will be time for my first lunch."

"Your first lunch?" said Poop.

"Oh, yes. I have my human beans very well trained. I pretend to dislike everything they place in front of me. So they keep bringing me new treats and ever more delicious food. That Scaredy Cat is a genius."

"I beg to differ," I told the snooty and, frankly, rather obese cat. "I find him to be a cruel oppressor stifling our feline freedoms!"

"We're on a mission!" chirped Poop. "To free Strawberry Lane from the evil influence of Scaredy Cat!"

"Won't you join our cause, friend?" I pleaded. "It's time to throw off your chains!"

"First of all, I'm not your friend. Having feline friends is against Scaredy Cat's rules. And second of all—how dare you call my necklace a chain? These are real jewels!"

"What is your name?" I asked, frustration filling my voice.

"Mister Cookiepants."

"Seriously?" said Poop.

"Seriously. Mister Fuzzface Greeneyes Cookiepants the Third, Esquire. And this is my housemate. His name is Bruno."

A hulking bulldog stepped out from behind the kitchen island and started huffing heavily. Strings of gooey drool were dangling off his jowls.

"Bruno and I have worked out an arrangement," said Mister Cookiepants. "I give him half of my food; he doesn't chase me."

"But," chortled Bruno with a slobbery chuckle, "that doesn't mean I can't chase other cats—like youse two!"

Chapter 18

Ohmigosh, ohmigosh, ohmigosh!

I thought I'd have a heart attack.

The bulldog bulldozed open the screen door and came charging after Pasha and me.

This was my first-ever dog chase. Oh, I'd heard about them. I'd seen them on cartoons inside the television. But to actually have a fire-breathing, snot-snorting bulldog chasing after me? My legs were limper than a mushy carrot-shaped catnip toy.

Fortunately, probably due to divine intervention, Bruno was soon distracted.

"Squirrel!" he shouted. He slammed on his brakes and plowed up some sod with his skidding front paws. Then he was off after the squirrel. Until he saw a bird. And then a bunny rabbit. Bruno wasn't big on maintaining focus. He chased after the next thing that moved, including a lawn ornament's windmill blades.

His lack of concentration allowed Pasha and me to slip into the next home to the right. It had a flapping pet door around back and we weren't afraid to use it. In fact, we sort of dove through the thing... together.

When we landed on the other side, we saw a string bean of a tiger-striped tabby kitten hanging upside down from a kitchen stool.

"Hi, guys!" it *meep*ed. "I'm Luigi. I'm three months old. You want to chase reflections on the wall? Oooh. There goes one. Hey. It moved. Just when I was going to swat it. Do either of you guys chase bubbles in seltzer water? I do. I haven't caught one yet. But one day, I will! Oooh! Light dot. On the wall."

"I take it you are new to the neighborhood?" said Pasha.

"Oh, yeah. Came here last week. Do you guys see any pens? I need to knock a pen off a countertop."

"Why?" I asked.

"Just to see if it will fall to the floor!"

"Good for you," said Pasha. "You're young. You're eager to learn."

"It's what I do. Twenty-four-seven. Everything is so wonderful! I know how to bury my poop in the litter box so no one will ever know I was there!"

"Have you met the Scaredy Cat?" I asked.

"The whoozee whatzee?"

"Scaredy Cat. Kind of scary-looking. Glowing orange eyes. Likes to dress up in spooky costumes?"

"Nope," said Luigi. "But I'm looking forward to it. I like meeting cats. Like you guys. What're your names?"

"I'm Poop."

The kitten giggled.

"Wow! That is so cool. I know how to poop but I've never known a Poop! See? This is why I love life. You can learn something new every day, especially if you've only been around for ninety of 'em."

"Come along, Poop," said Pasha with a sigh. "I don't believe Little Luigi is quite ready to join us in our cause."

"You want me to join you in your claws?" said Luigi. "Ouch. That might hurt. I got one of my claws stuck in the carpet the other day. I thought it was a very clever cat trap. Then my human beans unsnagged me. We all had a good laugh. Hee, hee, hee."

"If Scaredy Cat drops by," I told Luigi, "ignore him. He's just a big bully."

"Oh. Okay."

A car rumbled down Strawberry Lane, sending up a swirl of hubcap reflections. Luigi made himself dizzy chasing and leaping after them.

"Woo-hoo! Light dots!"

And while the kitten scampered, capered, skipped, and romped about, Pasha and I exited out the floppy pet door we'd so recently entered through.

"Finding recruits is harder than I thought it would be," I told Pasha as we slogged across the damp lawn.

"Don't give up, Poop. We have only just begun."

"Yeah. And so far, we have one definite no and one who definitely doesn't even know what we're talking about."

"Not to worry," said Pasha. "I am certain we will soon encounter a kindred spirit. Someone who wishes to overthrow Scaredy Cat as much as we do."

And wouldn't you know it?

Two minutes later, we met Ermine.

PASHA

Chapter 19

We were promenading (that, of course, means "walking") up the sidewalk.

I had my tail held high, expressing confidence and contentment. Poop, on the other paw, had her tail tucked away—curved beneath her body, signaling fear or submission. Something was making her nervous.

"What is it, Poop?" I asked.

"That's a forest up there. With trees. The last time I was near trees, a scary cat with glowing orange eyeballs leapt out of the underbrush to terrify me. It was the same rainy night that my first human beans tossed me out of the house and I became homeless."

"Fear not, Poop," I told her. "I am right here with you. Should anything leap out of the shrubbery, I—"

I was unable to complete that thought.

Because a crazed brown clump with splayed claws leapt out of the shrubbery.

Poop was so terrified, she immediately shrieked and puffed up her body as if it were a fur balloon.

The oversized lint ball that had just tumbled out of the brambles was a cat with matted fur, mud-streaked limbs, a snaggletooth, and a pinched-shut left eyeball! Yes, on second look, it was a cat. A tabby with the distinctive M mark on her forehead. It also appeared that our fellow feline was blind in one eye.

ERMINE

"Thorry!" she said as she found her legs and stood up. The snaggletooth jutting out of her upper jaw turned all her *s* sounds into *th*s. "Thought I was thwatting at a bumblebee. Didn't know I wath leaping. Definitely have thum depth pertheption and paw-eye coordination ith-youth going on here."

"What is your name?" I asked boldly, protectively positioning myself in front of Poop, who was hocking and wheezing as if she had asthma or the world's most irritating hairball.

"I'm Ermine," said the one-eyed cat. "I uthed to live in thith houthing project with the Jenkinth family. They rethcued me from a cat thelter even though, you know, I wathn't 'perfect' like Thcaredy Cat's favorite, Mithter Cookiepanth."

Ermine nodded toward that first house we'd visited earlier. The regal white cat was grooming himself on the sill of the living room window. His sparkling collar glinted in the sun.

"In fact, I'm about ath far from perfect ath you can get."

She pointed her paw up at her squinched-shut eye and her oddly angled tooth.

"Eventually, my people turned on me. I wath there on what they call a two-week trial."

Poop shot me a bug-eyed look. Yes, we were also on a two-week trial. Was Ermine an example of what might happen to us if we were to fail our fourteen-day test?

I shuddered at the thought.

My fur doesn't look good caked in mud or matted.

Chapter 20

Ermine was such a sad-looking cat.

She was also kind of hard to understand, on account of the snaggletooth poking out of her upper lip.

And the missing eyeball? Creepy. But Pasha was treating her with dignity and respect. I figured I could try to do the same.

"So, uh, why did your people 'turn on you'?'" I asked.

Ermine explained how her human beans thought she had repeatedly trashed their home and broken several of their favorite things, including an antique lava lamp and some porcelain figurines.

"Only, it wathn't me," Ermine told us. "It wath the Thcaredy Cat."

"I know!" I told her. "The Scaredy Cat is trying to do the same thing to our house. Only, Pasha and I are extremely lucky. Our human bean children cleaned everything up."

"Indeed they did," added Pasha. "Lance and Ash are the best."

"Kidth are thweet like that," said Ermine. "Unfortunately, the Jenkinthes only had a toddler in a playpen. Hith name was Tham."

"You mean Sam?"

"Yeth. That'th what I thaid. Tham. You thould've theen the meth Thcaredy Cat made in that houth."

I nodded slowly as I translated the mangled sentence to "You should've seen the mess Scaredy Cat made in that house."

"So your human beans tossed you out of the house?" I asked. "Because that's what my first humans did. They grabbed me by the scruff of the neck and heaved me out the back door into the damp and dreary rain!"

Ermine shook her head. "My humanth didn't do that. I, bathically, ran away becauth Thcaredy Cat banithed me to the woodth. He told me I wath

92

imperfect. On account of my thcrunched-up eye and my thnaggletooth here. And, according to Thcaredy Cat, thith thubdivithion ith only meant for perfect cath. I remember his wordth eggthactly..."

Maybe it was because Pasha and I had heard Scaredy Cat speak and threaten and bully before, but when Ermine assumed the voice of Scaredy Cat, it seemed as though her snaggletooth lisp completely disappeared. It was as if she were a ventriloquist's dummy and Scaredy Cat was directly speaking through her: "You are a misfit, Ermine. A freak. You are not a proper cat. In fact, you are an embarrassment to all of cat-kind. You must go live in the woods and never return!"

And that's what Ermine did. Because Scaredy Cat had convinced her that no human home—on Strawberry Lane or anywhere else—would want such a "deformed, imperfect, and defective" cat.

In the forest, she found a feral colony of similarly exiled creatures—none of whom knew where their next meal might come from. They just knew it would no longer be delivered in a nice bowl with water on the side. All of them had been evicted from the subdivision by Scaredy Cat, who, according to Ermine, wears the long black hooded robe of the

Grim Reaper whenever he goes about his banishment business.

"Be careful," Ermine warned us. "Or you will wind up like me. Living in the woodth with all the other thray cath. "

And, she informed us, there were hundreds of them.

All banished and living wretched, pitiful, and dangerous lives that no cat should ever have to live.

Especially me.

PASHA

Chapter 21

While Poop and Ermine chatted, I studied our new friend's unfortunate dental situation.

Actually, Ermine's mouth was in pretty good shape, except for that one snaggletooth up top.

Fortunately, I knew how to fix it. First of all, it appeared to be quite loose. I could only assume that the foods one had to eat in the wild were not as soft and mushy as the canned foods Poop and I were currently enjoying on a regular basis. Something Ermine had bitten into had, undoubtedly, jarred the tooth out of its socket and made it wobbly.

Secondly, as I explained earlier, the professor I lived with for four years had an endless selection of books in his library, including one entitled *Feline Dentistry: Oral Assessment, Treatment, and Preventative Care*. And believe it or not, in our very first year together, I had taught myself to read (silently, of course) by scanning the words printed on the pages as the professor read books out loud to me. I used that skill to skim through the dentistry textbook.

"Ermine?" I said.

"Yeth?"

"Would you like to have that snaggletooth extracted?"

"More than anything!"

"Very well. Poop? Would you kindly scurry back to our house and grab that ball of string you and Ash were playing with last night?"

"You're going to yank out her snaggletooth?" exclaimed Poop.

I nodded. "If our new friend is agreeable."

"Oh, yeth, pleath! I'm tired of talking like thith!"

"But aren't you afraid it'll hurt?" asked Poop.

"'Do the thing you fear,'" I proclaimed, quoting Ralph Waldo Emerson, "'and the death of fear is certain!'"

"I agree!" shouted Ermine. "Let'th do thith thing!"

Poop scampered home to retrieve the string. I talked Ermine through her upcoming procedure. When Poop returned, I looped the string around Ermine's wobbly tooth and told her to hug a nearby fire hydrant. Tightly. Meanwhile, I wrapped the loose end of the string around my front paw.

"Ready?" I inquired.

"Ready!" Ermine shouted back.

I blasted off like a thunderbolt, running up the sidewalk as fast as I could.

Ten seconds and a good yank later, the snaggle-tooth popped free!

"Thank you!" gushed Ermine. She quickly tried out her new dental arrangement. "Six socks sit in a sink, soaking in soapsuds!" She whistled a little, but her voice was strong and clear. "This is fantastic."

I, of course, was beaming. "You see, Poop? When we overcome our fears, we can accomplish so much!"

"That's the truth, Pasha!" cried Ermine, doing a little happy cat dance.

"Hey, Ermine," said Poop, "since Pasha helped you, do you want to help us overthrow Scaredy Cat?"

"Excuse me?"

"We are organizing a resistance movement," I

said. "We want to get all the cats currently living on Strawberry Lane to stand up to Scaredy Cat. There are more of us than there are of him. And if we succeed, no cat will ever have to face the banishment to the woods that you had to face. You could help us make the argument."

"Um, I'm not so sure," said Ermine. "I mean, look at me. I'm a mess. Yes, my snaggletooth is gone, but I haven't licked myself clean in months. And this squinty eye? It scares cats. People, too. I should probably just head back to the woods."

Ermine started trotting up the cul-de-sac. Poop and I trotted right behind her.

"Please?" said Poop. "Pretty please with a scoop of tuna on top?"

"No. It's too scary."

"You have nothing to fear but fear itself!" I shouted to the scampering cat.

Trotting behind the terrified tangle of matted fur, we rounded a slight curve on a section of Strawberry Lane that Poop and I had not yet explored. There was a thick clump of woods to our left. Ermine slammed on her brakes and skidded to a halt in front of a spooky stone house shaded by so many trees that it looked like perpetual night had fallen on the small home.

"We went too far!" she said, her voice trembling.

"Too far?" I asked. "This is still Strawberry Lane, is it not?"

Ermine nodded nervously. "Yes. The golf course is just beyond those trees. And this? This is *the caretaker's cottage*!"

The way she said it? Dramatic *DUN-DUN-DUN* music was ringing in my ears!

Chapter 22

I don't believe in haunted houses.

But then again, up until I saw the thing with the orange glowy eyes near a garbage can, I didn't believe in Scaredy Cats, either. Oh, sure, I'd heard of them. Scaredy Cats are the stuff of legend. Kitty tales. The kind of story your parents might tell you at bedtime when you're a kitten to scare you into doing what's right.

"Finish your breakfast or Scaredy Cat will gobble you up. Pee in the box or Scaredy Cat will bury you in a sandbox. Stay away from dogs or Scaredy Cat will turn you into a tug toy." Stuff like that. Of course, we kittens are only with our moms for a few weeks before we're shipped off to shelters or forever homes. But those early Scaredy Cat warnings? They stick with you.

Anyway, the caretaker's cottage, as Ermine called it? Spooky and creepy to the max. It was like something straight out of a haunted Halloween special inside the TV.

It had a steeply gabled roof and ivy-covered walls made out of stone.

"That's Loach's house," whispered Ermine.

"Who's Loach?" I asked.

"The caretaker."

"Really?" sniffed Pasha. "Well, he doesn't take very good care of his house. Vine-y things are growing on all its walls. And just look at those rusty wrought iron bars in the windows."

"Loach is the caretaker for the golf course," explained Ermine. "This used to be the grounds-keeper's cottage for his mother's entire estate. Her name was Helga von Bumbottom. Years ago, she owned all this land. Everything. As far as my eye can see. The golf course. Strawberry Lane. All the houses? They sit on what used to be von Bumbottom property. She sold it all to the real estate developers, except for this cottage. When she passed away, this tumbledown stone house was the only thing Loach inherited. All of Mrs. von Bumbottom's money—millions and millions of dollars—went to building a cat art museum that nobody goes to. It's mostly oil paintings and portraits of cats."

"I suspect Mrs. von Bumbottom simply wished to teach her son how to be self-reliant," said Pasha. "She undoubtedly wanted Loach to make his own way in this world and not have everything handed to him on a silver platter."

"Nah," said Ermine. "She was just mean. Nasty,

too. A real perfectionist. Everything had to be just so. She made Loach comb the grass in their front lawn so all the blades were facing the same way. At least that's what I heard from Old Lenny." Ermine gestured toward the woods. "Lenny's the wisest cat in my feral colony."

"Are there any cats currently residing at this address?" asked Pasha, eager to find more recruits for our Scaredy Cat resistance movement.

"In the caretaker's cottage?" said Ermine. "No way. Loach hates cats. Probably because his mother loved hers so much. Lenny told me that Mrs. von Bumbottom used to yell at Loach and tell him he wasn't good enough to scoop her cat's poop."

"Poor kid," I said.

"Yeah," said Ermine. "It warped him. Warped him good. So steer clear of the caretaker's cottage. Unless you want to end up on the business end of a water hose!"

"No, thank you," said Pasha.

"We're cats," I told Ermine. "We hate being sprayed with water."

Ermine nodded. "And that's exactly why Loach does it. *He* hates cats."

PASHA

Chapter 23

"So, Pasha," said Ermine as the three of us pranced down the street. "You guys really want to meet a bunch of cats banished to the woods for all eternity by Scaredy Cat?"

"Indeed we do," I assured her. "Perhaps we can convert them to our cause. There is strength in numbers. It's why dictators and tyrants fear the masses so much. We must educate as many cats as possible. For, as a wise human bean named Robespierre once said, 'The secret of freedom lies in educating people, whereas the secret of tyranny is in keeping them ignorant.'"

"Did the professor read that to you?" asked Poop.

I nodded. "Constantly."

"Okay," said Ermine. "Come with me."

"Where?" asked Poop. I could hear the fear in her voice. "Not some new spooky place, because, IMHO, that caretaker's cottage was enough creepiness for one day."

"I want you two to meet my family. The colony of banished cats."

"They're in the woods, correct?" I asked.

"Yep," said Ermine.

"Oh, joy," said Poop. "Love me some woods." She was being sarcastic, of course.

We traipsed through the brambles and underbrush and entered a cool, dark world of towering evergreen trees and soft pillows of pine needles beneath our paws. I thought the woods were spectacular and nicely pine-scented. Poop thought they were yucky. And scary.

"What was that?" she asked repeatedly.

One time it was a hoot owl. Another time, a croaking frog. Another, it was Ermine. Passing gas.

After a few minutes, following a well-worn pawpath, we reached a clearing. There was a circle of stones in the center.

"This is our meeting place," explained Ermine.

"We don't meet up as a group all that often. Just when we have visitors or a new banished cat to greet. Most days, it's every cat for themselves out here. We have to forage for food. Nobody's going to bring it to us in a shiny bowl. We have to hunt real rodents instead of make-believe fur mice."

"Gross," muttered Poop. "Don't you guys have Fancy Feast Marinated Morsels out here? Healthy Gourmet Paté? Grain-Free Weruva?"

"Hardly," scoffed Ermine. "Last night? I ate two crunchy bugs and nibbled on a stick."

"Disgusting," said Poop.

"It's how we survive," grumbled a cat behind us.

We turned around. A very mangled, very angry tomcat came prowling out of the evergreens. He was followed by a hodgepodge of equally mangy and mangled creatures. Cats with stubby tails. Missing eyes. Limps. They all had extremely serious expressions or snarls on their faces. Most of their tails were pointing straight down to signal aggression. A few tails were slapping back and forth rapidly—indicating fear and a willingness to attack.

It was clear. None of Ermine's friends were happy to see Poop and me.

"Sorry to disturb," I said with a friendly smile.

ERMINE'S FELINE FOREST FRIENDS

"But you did anyway," said the leader, settling down in front of me on his haunches so he could burn me with an angry glare.

"My name is Pasha," I said as pleasantly as I could. "This is my housemate, Poop."

Poop curtsied awkwardly. "Charmed, I'm sure."

"I'm K," said the leader of the feral cats. "*K* for 'Cat.'"

I nodded. "Riiiiiight."

It made no sense to correct his spelling. Very few

cats are familiar with the workings of the human bean alphabet.

"I don't have a housemate," K hissed. "You know why? Because I don't have a house! Scaredy Cat took it away from me, two years ago!"

Chapter 24

It was so sad to hear about what happened to K because, honestly, it could soon happen to me!

Pasha, too!

Ermine encouraged K to tell us more.

"The brainy one, Pasha, extracted my snaggle-tooth," she said. "He's very, very smart."

"And I'm a good listener," I said, because, well, I am. Especially when I'm listening to the TV or a good story.

"Fine," said the crusty K. "Oh, I was living the high life. Right there on Strawberry Lane. I had me one of those carpeted cat trees with all the perches and the tetherballs. Very posh. Very comfy. Three times a day, my human beans brought me tender vittles. Dainty morsels of fish or chicken..."

All the other wild cats were suddenly licking their lips and purring. All of them remembering a similar past.

"They would scoop my litter and keep it fresh. All I had to do was, every now and then, purr or meow or do something cute. I slept a lot. I ate a lot. I licked my fur. I followed my human beans around from room to room and wove in and out between their legs."

Now all the other cats sighed.

"Those were the days," said one.

"But then," continued K, "Scaredy Cat came to call. He just appeared in my sunny living room. One minute he's a ghostly reflection inside the big picture window. The next, he's patrolling across the back of the couch, all dressed up like a police officer."

"Then what happened?" I asked, my eyes wide. K's visit from Scaredy Cat was sounding eerily similar to one of ours.

"'What's this I hear about your peculiar behavior?' the horrible creature hissed at me. 'Are you some sort of deviant?' Of course, I had no idea what a deviant was. So Scaredy Cat explained. 'You have

CAPT. SCAREDY CAT

been departing from usual and accepted standards of cattiness. Following your human from room to room? That's what dogs do, not cats.'"

Now all the cats hissed.

"What happened next?" I asked.

"Scaredy Cat trashed my home. He scattered kitty litter all over the floor—including several clods of congealed poop. He knocked over my climbing tree. He broke my lady's favorite glass figurines. He dumped kibble pellets all over the floor."

"Your human beans must've been angry," said Pasha.

"Oh, they were. They wondered what had come over me. The lady told the man that I must have 'issues.' They took me to see a cat psychiatrist. Well, actually, she was human, but she specialized in cats with behavioral issues. After that, they hired a trainer. But Scaredy Cat ruined everything. He kept coming to the house, destroying more precious objects. After a few months of mayhem, my human beans had no choice. They planned on returning me to the animal shelter where they'd rescued me, even though I had, supposedly, been their family cat for three years."

"On Strawberry Lane?" I asked, wondering why it took Scaredy Cat so long to start tormenting K.

"Nah," said K. "The first two and a half years we lived over on Montague Street. And back then, my name was Fluffy Cuddles. Anyway, Scaredy Cat came to visit me one last time—right around midnight. He was all dressed up in a hooded black robe that seemed to waft in the breeze even though there wasn't any breeze to waft it.

"Scaredy Cat looked at me with those great big glowing orange eyeballs and said, 'You have reached the end of the line, Fluffy Cuddles. Your human beans are going to take you back to the shelter. And since you are no longer a kitten but, rather, a full-grown, pampered cat, I guarantee that you will never find a new home.' That's when Scaredy Cat gave me the option of living by his rules, swearing my allegiance, or running away into eternal banishment. I went with the banishment option. Hey, it beats living a lie or living behind bars in a cage until someone decides to give you the big needle. That was three years ago. I changed my name to K for Cat, because it was easier to spell than Fluffy Cuddles. I've been out here in the wilderness ever since."

"And Scaredy Cat leaves you alone?" I asked.

"Oh, he stops by from time to time to gloat. He still tries to scare us. But to tell you the truth, he's nothing compared to what we have to be afraid of out here. There's all sorts of predators roaming around in the woods, looking for a quick snack of cat."

Suddenly, I heard a bunch of high-pitched barks and yips blending into a howling song.

K nudged his head toward where the yipping had come from. "For instance, that guy? He's a coyote. And guess what? He's very, very hungry."

PASHA

Chapter 25

"A coyote?" I said.

K shrugged. "Welcome to the wild, Mr. Smarty-pants. You want to go extract one of his teeth?"

"No, thank you." I turned to Poop. "Well, I suppose we should be heading home."

She nodded eagerly. In fact, she was working her head up and down so rapidly, I was afraid it might fly off.

"Nice to meet you guys," she said. "Ermine? We have to do this again. Except the deep woods part. We could skip that part. Pasha? You and I need to skedaddle. Now."

"Indeed we do," I told the herd of abandoned

cats. "Pleasure meeting all of you. We'll be back."

"Why?" asked K.

"We're putting together an action plan for standing up to Scaredy Cat."

K laughed. "Ha! Sure you are."

The coyote yipped and yapped in the distance.

"Buh-bye, everybody!" said Poop as she took off running.

I was right behind her.

We didn't follow the well-worn path this time. We just ran. Away from the coyote. Away from the cat clowder (that's what you call a group of cats), who'd started to scatter just like us. Soon Poop and I found ourselves in a thick stand of trees. The trees bordered an open green field. We dashed across it and headed uphill, where we had to avoid an oval of sand.

"Where'd the sand come from?" cried Poop.

"Who knows?" I replied. "Perhaps the beach."

We clambered up a grassy knoll and came to a neatly trimmed circle of grass.

"It's a lawn!" Poop shouted with joy. "I've never been so happy to be on a well-manicured lawn before in my life."

All of a sudden, a bouncy white ball fell out of

the sky. It hit the clipped grass and rolled downhill to a hole with a waving flag stuck into it.

"I believe we're on the golf course!" I shouted. "We need to find our way back to Strawberry Lane!"

We took off running again, just as a golf cart puttered up an asphalt path.

Mr. Wilde was riding in it.

"Whoa. Pasha? Poop?" he shouted after us as we raced across the fairway.

"Those your cats, Wilde?" we heard another man in the cart ask.

"Maybe. I mean, they kind of look like our cats. They're running away so fast it's hard to tell."

"Well, it's against club rules for cats to be on the course."

"Then it's a good thing I'm not a member of the club," we heard Mr. Wilde say with a laugh. "I'm just a guest."

"Rules apply to guests, too," grumbled the other man.

"I suppose they do. Now let's talk about that instrument you want me to build for you, Bob..."

Poop and I kept running.

Pretty soon, we were tearing through the thwacking underbrush.

"It's the creepy caretaker's cottage!" gasped Poop when we emerged from the thicket.

"No worries," I told her, panting for breath. "That means we are close to Strawberry Lane and home!"

"Do you think Mr. Wilde really recognized us?" asked Poop as we trotted up the street.

"It's a possibility. But I suspect he will soon forget all about our brief encounter on the fairway as he continues to chase the little white ball around the eighteen holes, ruining what would otherwise be a perfectly nice walk. Meanwhile, you and I, Poop, have eluded a wild coyote. And an incoming golf ball."

"You're right. We did."

"To do so took cunning and courage."

"Yeah," said Poop, puffing out her chest. "For the first time in my life, I'm feeling brave. I'm not afraid of anything."

"That's the spirit," I told her. "It's also the only way we'll ever defeat Scaredy Cat. Come on. There's home. I need to head in and grab a quick catnap."

"Me too."

We proudly romped around the house (*our* home!) and headed for the back door.

Where Scaredy Cat was waiting for us.

On the rear stoop.

This time, he was dressed in a pirate costume.

SCAREDY CAT

Chapter 26

Oh, the two cats looked so deliciously terrified.

Pasha and Poop.

Such cutesy-pootsy names for such wretched rebels. How dare they traipse around MY neighborhood, stirring up resistance and revolution?

They weren't expecting to find ME sitting outside their kitchen door, now, were they? Of course not. They fail to understand my many, many powers.

"I take it you met Ermine?" I said so coldly I gave myself raw-turkey-skin-sized goose bumps. "Perhaps I should lend her this eye patch. She needs it more than I."

Pasha and Poop both had their fur puffed up,

trying to look bigger, trying to intimidate ME! It wasn't working. Especially when Poop shivered. I knew she had just piddled in the yard.

"Did you meet K and the others? The banished cats in the woods?"

"Yes," said Pasha. "We most certainly did." He was doing his best to sound like a tough guy. It wasn't working.

"Did you enjoy their company?" I asked with a sneer and a hiss of a half laugh.

"It was okay," mumbled Poop. "I guess."

"And how about the food?" I asked gleefully. "Did they offer you a snack? A bit of mouse or bird, perhaps? Some wild mushrooms that might or might not have been poisonous?"

"We weren't hungry," said Pasha.

"Oh, but you will be when you join them. Unfortunately, K, Ermine, and the others aren't very generous with their provisions. You two will have to hunt and gather for yourselves. In time, you'll be pawing the earth, rooting around for grubworms."

"We're not going to the woods," said Pasha. "You can't banish us."

"True, I suppose. I usually need a human or two to threaten eviction first. Then the choice is yours.

Obey my edicts, be banished to the darkness of the woods, or face certain death at your friendly neighborhood kill shelter. Most agree to follow my rules and live happily ever after."

"We could get adopted again," muttered Poop.

"Foolish little girl." I laughed. "You are getting older and older every day. Uglier, too. Human beans only want cute, cuddly kittens—not tossed-out old coots like you two. If you go back to the animal shelter, you will never come out alive."

"Well," said Pasha, thrusting out his chest dramatically. "The Wildes love us. No way are they kicking us out of this house."

I smirked. "You and I will simply have to agree to disagree, Pasha," I told him. "However, if you fall in line, if you start paying me the homage I deserve, if you loyally obey my every command, I suspect that your human beans won't find cause to remove you from your comfortable and cushy home."

"And if we don't?" demanded Pasha. "If we refuse to surrender?"

Now all I could do was grin. His Captain Courageous act was so entertaining.

"If you don't do as I say, then everything you think you have could disappear in a *poof!*"

I snapped my claws. Sparks flew from my paw tips, followed by a puff of green smoke.

It's one of my best special effects.

"What did you just do?" gasped Poop.

"Something that can be undone just as quickly. IF you bend the knee and swear feline fidelity to me!"

"Never!" shouted Pasha. "Never, never, never!"

Now I just had to laugh.

"We shall see, Pasha. Never is *such* a long time." I stepped aside and gestured to their flapping cat door. "Welcome home. Good luck explaining what you two just did inside!"

Chapter 27

What we just did? I wondered.

We didn't do anything. Okay, I tinkled in the backyard, but, come on, squirrels and chipmunks and birds do that all the time.

The crazed Scaredy Cat threw back his head and laughed a villainous laugh. And then—*FWUMP!* He disappeared in another one of his clouds of green smoke.

"We didn't do anything inside," I said to Pasha. "Right?"

"Of course not," replied my friend. "We haven't even been inside yet. However, I suspect that Scaredy

Cat has made it *look* as if we did do something. And I further suspect it won't be pretty!"

Pasha dashed up the steps and flew through the floppy pet door. I dashed behind him.

When we hit the kitchen, we saw it.

Oh, the horror. The horror.

Once again, food was strewn everywhere. Cracked eggs. Glugging milk jugs lying on their sides. Melting pints of ice cream. The entire contents of the refrigerator had been emptied on the floor. A wilted head of lettuce was swimming in a pool of ketchup and mayonnaise and pickle juice.

Things were even worse in the living room.

"Yikes!" I screeched.

A very valuable antique Tiffany lamp—its shade a work of stained-glass art—lay shattered on the floor. The curio cabinet's doors had been swung open. Mrs. Wilde's collection of Disney character figurines was missing all its heads. Her ballerina music box, which, we'd been told, she'd had since she was a child, had been smashed—the ballerina snapped in half.

"The dastardly fiend!" shouted Pasha, shaking his fist at the ceiling.

"Mrs. Wilde is going to think we did all this!" I yelped. "Then, when Mr. Wilde tells her we were breaking rules by running around on the golf course..."

"Let us hope the children, Ash and Lance, return home before their parents," said Pasha. "They might be able to clean this mess up and protect us."

He started scurrying around, desperately trying to tidy up the living room. It was impossible. Cats don't have thumbs for picking things up. Or Krazy Glue for putting shattered figurines back together.

Suddenly, I heard a sloshing sound. Upstairs.

"What's that?" I wondered aloud.

"Water," said Pasha, taking the staircase steps two at a time. "It sounds like it's coming from one of the bathrooms on the second floor!"

There was a very loud *SPLASH* as a flood of water came cascading down the steps, transforming it into a waterfall.

"Scaredy Cat turned on the water faucet in the upstairs tub!" cried Pasha as he spun around and tried to outrun the tumbling tsunami rolling down the steps behind him. (We cats hate water, remember.)

That's when the living room ceiling started to dribble.

Water had soaked through the bathroom floor

and was now pitter-pattering through the plaster so fast it looked like the ceiling was sweating.

That's also when the front door swung open.

"Hey, guys. I'm home."

It was Mrs. Wilde. She dropped her keys into a bowl near the front door.

"Come on," said Pasha. "Put on your cutest kitten eyes. Follow me."

We scampered to the foyer and looked up at Mrs. Wilde with wide and woeful gazes. Pasha fluttered his eyebrows like butterfly wings. I rolled over on my back to show Mrs. Wilde my belly.

She smiled and gave me a playful rub.

"Whose good girl are you, huh? Whose good girl?"

Our distraction was working.

Until it wasn't.

Mrs. Wilde heard the trickling water, some of which was now pooling around her shoes. She saw the leaky ceiling. The shattered figurines. The crumpled music box.

"What the—"

She stepped into the living room. Where she froze. Because, from that spot, she could also see the destruction in the kitchen. And the steady drip of water leaking out of the ceiling.

Which exploded into a gusher.

She spun around and glared at Pasha and me.

Mrs. Wilde was not fluttering her eyes to give us cute kitty kisses. Oh, no. Her eyes were firing lethal laser beams!

PASHA

Chapter 28

"You two are disasters!" screamed Mrs. Wilde.

Then she sloshed her way up the stairs to deal with whatever faucet she thought we had nudged open.

"This is bad, Pasha," said Poop. "Real bad." She was, once again, trembling in fear.

"For goodness' sake," I warned her, "whatever you do, don't piddle on the carpet."

"Too late. But I did piddle in the puddle underneath the leaky ceiling. So..."

"We must acknowledge that what we did was wrong."

"But," protested Poop, "we didn't do anything. It

was Scaredy Cat. That snap-and-*poof* trick. The guy's like a wizard."

"I realize we are innocent," I told her. "But there is no way to pin this disaster on a magical, wizarding Scaredy Cat that's nowhere to be seen. All we can do, Poop, is beg and plead for forgiveness. Put on your most piteous face."

Mrs. Wilde came stomping down the squishy staircase.

At the bottom of the steps, I made my eyes go wide, went up on my haunches, and clutched my paws in front of my chest. Poop did the same.

We ain't too proud to beg... for forgiveness.

"You broke my music box, too?" Mrs. Wilde was near tears when she said that. Oh, for a voice to explain. All we could do was mewl and squeak in shame as water *drip-plink-drip*ped from the ceiling. "And my Disney figurines."

Mrs. Wilde shook her head.

"You two may not last one week in this house, let alone two!"

When she said that, I could feel my heart breaking. I have never felt so ashamed. Not even when I was living in the gutters and back alleys of St. Petersburg. The one in Russia. Not Florida. If cats could blush, my white fur would've turned a deep shade of pink.

For the first time, the power of Scaredy Cat was becoming crystal clear. By whatever terrifying powers he possessed, he was in a position to ruin our lives. Forever.

Mrs. Wilde shook her head and pointed toward the back door.

"Bad cats! Bad, bad, bad!"

I gasped. I couldn't believe that this was happening. Mrs. Wilde was shooing us out of the house. I have never been shooed out before. Trust me, it's not a great feeling.

Our tails tucked between our legs, our heads drooping in shame, Poop and I plodded across the kitchen (attempting to avoid the mayonnaise oil slick and the pickle juice puddles) and crawled in disgrace through the floppy pet door.

"We're doomed!" cried Poop the instant we were outside. "No one has ever called me a bad cat before. Even my first human beans, when they tossed me out, didn't say I was bad. They just said I had the wrong color fur."

"I beg your pardon?"

"It was an interior decorating thing. I clashed with their new palette. Pasha?"

"Yes, Poop?"

"You're the smartest cat I've ever met."

"I hear that a lot…"

"So tell me: Are we officially banished? Do we have to go live in the woods now?"

I shook my head. "No. I think this is one of those bumps in the road that the Wilde family will look back on one day and laugh."

The kitchen door flew open.

Mrs. Wilde was standing there. Her hair was wet and spackled from where another chunk of the living room ceiling must've collapsed on her.

"Bad, bad cats!" she hollered.

Poop and I bolted up and over the backyard's stockade fence.

We needed to stay away from Mrs. Wilde until she cooled down and was ready to look back on all this and laugh about our cute, kittenish antics.

I figured it might take a day. Maybe a week. Maybe longer.

Until then, Poop and I would have to fend for ourselves.

Chapter 29

We made our way, like the tightrope walkers I'd seen on TV, along the narrow railings atop the fences penning in all the homes on Strawberry Lane.

Pasha was in the lead.

"I suggest we return to the golf course," he said over his shoulder. "It might be a good source of garbage cans and salvageable food."

"Garbage cans?" I whined.

"Yes. From my studies of golf, there are often outdoor dining establishments near the clubhouse. Dumpsters brimming with uneaten food."

"Gross."

"It's how I survived in Russia."

We hopped off the fence, trotted across Straw-berry Lane, and approached the creepy caretaker's house.

Ermine was there. It looked like she'd been wait-ing for us.

"Hi, guys," she said cheerlessly. "We heard what happened."

"You did?" I said, sounding surprised, because I was.

"Yeah. Scaredy Cat came to our meeting place in the woods. Told us to 'expect company.' He said you two were about to be given the heave-ho by your human beans."

"Not officially," said Pasha. "However, we were labeled 'bad cats' for the first time in our lives."

Ermine nodded. "That's how it starts. Next thing you know, *BOOM!* They're stuffing you in cat carriers for the long ride back to the nearest animal shelter."

"Well," said Pasha with a sigh, "we're definitely not going to live by Scaredy Cat's rules. I suppose we could run away and join you and your colleagues in the wild."

"Yeah. That's usually how it goes. At least Scaredy Cat gives you choices. So he's not all bad..."

"He's worse than bad!" I cried out. "He's evil.

Ruining perfectly happy cat homes, just because we won't live by all of his stupid rules? I don't want to be aloof and cold. I like cuddling with Ash at night!"

"So," said Ermine, "you guys are still rebelling against him, huh?"

"With all our might," said Pasha, fuming. "This is not normal. Scaredy Cat must be defeated, by any means necessary."

"Well," said Ermine, "you might want to—"

She stopped. Abruptly.

Because someone had just puttered up the driveway of the creepy caretaker's cottage in a rattling and dented golf cart. He had a bag of antique clubs jangling in the cargo hold.

"It's Loach!" whispered Ermine.

"Cats!" Loach hissed, reaching over his shoulder to grab the bulging wooden head of a club. "I hate cats!"

Loach leapt out of the cart and, swinging the weapon wildly over his head, charged across the lawn.

"You've been peeing in my rhododendron bushes, making them stink, haven't you?"

He took a swing at Ermine. She quickly sprang to her left and avoided the *whoosh*ing wooden head of the club.

Pasha shot out his fur, made an extremely angry face, and hissed.

"What?" said Loach. "You want some of this, Snowball?"

Another swing. Another miss.

"You guys?" I shouted. "Let's get out of here."

I bolted for the underbrush. Pasha and Ermine were right behind me.

Loach grabbed a garden hose and trained its nozzle at our bobbing tails.

He squirted me good. Right in my butt.

"What a slovenly, foul-smelling creep!" said the panting Pasha once we were safely hidden in the shadows of the trees ringing the golf course. "An ignoramus if ever I saw one. An ignorant oaf. A boorish idiot!"

"True," said Ermine. "But everybody has their story. Even Loach. And when you hear that story, well, sometimes you figure out why a creature acts the way it does."

And that's when she told us how Loach became, well, *Loach*.

PASHA

Chapter 30

Poop and I settled into what golfers call the rough—
the fringe of untamed forest ringing their well-
clipped golfing lawn.

Ermine paced back and forth in front of us, ready
to reveal Loach's history.

"Like I told you, Loach's family, the von Bum-
bottoms, used to own all this land. They had a
fruit orchard. Mostly strawberries, blueberries, and
apples."

"Is that how our cul-de-sac came to be known as
Strawberry Lane?" I asked.

"Yeah. Anyway, Loach's mother and father
worked him hard. Made him pick fruit, trim limbs,

spread fertilizer. In the summer, of course, he didn't have to go to school, so he could easily help out in the orchards. But his parents took him out of school in the fall, too, for apple-picking time. It's why Loach was held back so often. He finally graduated with a junior high school diploma when he was seventeen."

"Poor fellow," I said. "Learning is the key to a brighter future."

"Which is why Loach's parents didn't want him learning anything. They didn't care about his future. They just wanted cheap labor. In time, Loach's father passed away. Loach thought things might get easier. Instead, they got worse. Like I told you, Mrs. von Bumbottom was a real perfectionist. If a piece of rotten fruit fell anywhere in the orchard, Loach had to go pick it up. No matter the hour. Mrs. von Bumbottom liked a tidy orchard. Then came Ebenezer."

"Who was Ebenezer?" I asked.

"Mrs. von Bumbottom's cat," said Ermine. "All the love Mother Loach might've given to her son, she showered on that cat. Pampered him. Bought him all sorts of costumes. Liked to dress him up. Sent his picture in to all the cat calendars. Fifteen years ago, Ebenezer was Mr. March in the Cat Lady Wall Calendar. Made their datebook, too. Ebenezer ate out of crystal goblets at the dining room table with Mrs. von Bumbottom while her son, Loach, had to eat slop out of a soup bowl with a wooden spoon in the kitchen. She even made him sit on the floor."

As Ermine continued her tale, the sun started slipping down toward the horizon on the far side of the golf course. The trees were darkening. The air cooling. It would soon be night and Poop and I would, most likely, have no place to sleep. Well, no place indoors. (I predicted that Mrs. Wilde would remain angry at us for at least forty-eight hours, if not longer.)

"I guess it's no wonder Loach hates cats," said Poop with a sigh.

"So what became of Ebenezer?" I asked.

"He, like all cats must, passed away," replied Ermine. "He lived to be twenty."

I whistled. Twenty is an impressive age for a cat. I'm aiming for twenty-five.

"Heartbroken, Loach's mother passed away six months after her beloved cat," Ermine went on. "That was only one week after she became a multimillionaire, selling off most of her land to the real estate developers who built these housing subdivisions and the deluxe eighteen-hole golf course."

"And none of that real estate money went to Loach?" I asked.

Ermine shook her head. "All he received was the caretaker cottage, his mother's collection of framed paintings and photographs, and the guarantee of a lifetime minimum-wage job as the golf course's groundskeeper. And to keep the cottage, he had to hang up all sorts of framed photographs of his mother or Mrs. von Bumbottom's lawyer would've taken the house away from him, too."

Poop and I shook our heads and sighed. In the silence, I could've sworn I heard Ash and Lance off in the distance.

"Pasha?" they cried. "Poop? Where are you guys?"

"Mom is sorry she got mad at you!" hollered Lance.

"Please come home!" screamed Ash. She had a very loud rock'n'roll voice. "Now! I mean it!"

"Do you hear that, Pasha!" Poop chirped eagerly. "They want us to come home!"

"And so we shall, Poop. Thank you, Ermine, for this information about Loach's pedigree."

"Huh?" said Ermine.

Poop rolled her eyes. "He means, 'Thanks for telling us about Loach.'"

I bristled slightly. "That's precisely what I said, Poop."

"Pasha?" cried Lance.

"Poop?" shouted Ash.

"See you tomorrow, Ermine!" said Poop with a huge grin. "Pasha and I are going home!"

Chapter 31

Pasha and I scampered out of the woods.

"There you are!" shouted Lance.

"Come here, pretty kitty!" added Ash.

Both of the Wilde children crouched down and threw open their arms. I ran to Ash first, weaving in and out of her legs, rubbing my fur up against her jeans. Pasha did the same with Lance. Then we switched partners. It was like a do-si-do in a square dance.

"You guys had us, like, totally worried," said Lance.

"Don't ever run away again!" added Ash.

Um, we didn't run away, I wanted to say. *We were*

shooed out the door. But I didn't say any of that. I just purred contentedly. I sounded like a miniature motorboat.

"Mom knows you guys didn't trash the house," said Lance.

I arched a quizzical eyebrow to say *She does?*

"It was a raccoon," added Ash.

"Dad told Mom he saw you two dudes tearing across the golf course this afternoon," said Lance. "He thought that was hysterical, even if his clients didn't. Anyway, if you were off playing golf, no way could you have torn up the house like that. You guys have an alibi."

I looked to Pasha.

"That means we have an excuse," Pasha whispered to me. "According to Mr. Wilde, we were somewhere else when the offense was committed."

"That's good," I whispered back. "Right?"

"No," said Pasha with a grin. "It's excellent."

"It was a raccoon," Ash said again.

She and Ash started strolling up the sidewalk toward home. Pasha and I eagerly followed after them. Yes, it was very doggish of us. I think I even wagged my tail with joy. We were in direct violation of about a half dozen of Scaredy Cat's rules.

"Dad says the raccoon snuck in through your pet door," said Lance. "Did all that damage in the kitchen. Then it ran upstairs and turned on both faucets in the bathtub."

"Raccoons are very good with their hands," said Ash. "They could totally shred a guitar solo." She made wild finger-twiddling motions with both hands. I think they call it playing air guitar."

"So while we went searching for you guys," explained Lance, "Dad ran over to the home improvement store to get one of those big plastic owls. One with a solar-powered head that moves. He says it'll scare off anything. Mice. Birds. Maybe even raccoons."

Mr. and Mrs. Wilde were waiting on the front porch.

"You found them!" gushed Mrs. Wilde, sounding super relieved.

"Yeah," said Lance. "They were in the woods. Over near the golf course."

Mr. Wilde laughed. "You guys love golf, huh?"

Pasha and I both meowed, as if to say, *Yes. Yes, we do.*

All the Wildes were beaming as we practically

hopped up the front steps and sashayed into the foyer.

"The insurance company will take care of this mess," said Mr. Wilde.

"And I'm so sorry I got so upset about a silly antique lamp," said Mrs. Wilde, bending down to give us each a good chin rubbing. "It's just a thing. Sure, it's been in my family for like a hundred years, but you two *are* family."

"You're their fur babies," teased Lance. "That's what Mom called you."

The Wildes all laughed. They did a lot of that. Pasha and I headed into the kitchen for a feast. Real chicken. Real tuna. Real human-bean-grade food!

While we waited for the kids to give us freeze-dried salmon treats for dessert, Pasha and I gazed out a window into the backyard.

We saw the head-bobbing plastic owl. Mr. Wilde had set it up on a stump illuminated by a misty floodlight.

"You think that thing will really work against raccoons?" I wondered out loud.

"Doubtful," said Pasha. "Raccoons are fearless. You have to chase them off by banging pots and pans.

But, if I may, our new artificial owl does seem to be doing an excellent job warding off Scaredy Cat."

"What?!?"

Pasha gestured toward a shadowy spot near the rear fence. I could see two glowing orange eyeballs.

"Apparently," said Pasha, "Mr. Wilde has accidentally stumbled upon the one thing that our Scaredy Cat might actually be scared of."

It was true.

The orange eyeballs seemed to shimmy in the darkness. As if Scaredy Cat were trembling. Hadn't he heard? "The thing you fear most has no power. Your fear of it is what has the power."

And right now, that plastic owl was the most powerful creature on Strawberry Lane!

"He can be defeated," said Pasha. "He will be defeated. Poop, my friend?"

"Yes, Pasha?"

"This is war!"

PASHA

Chapter 32

The next morning, things were, of course, chaotic in the Wilde house.

Mr. Wilde was tuning a guitar with one hand while slurping cereal with the other. Mrs. Wilde was doing finger painting. On a kitchen wall. She wanted to test-run a decorating idea she had for her Good Earth preschool kids.

Lance, the artist and sculptor, was helping his mother by molding oatmeal clumps and sticking them on the swirl-painted wall.

"Awesome," said Mrs. Wilde, painting over the oatmeal, incorporating it into her piece.

(I wondered if the insurance company would also pay to have the kitchen wall repaired.)

Meanwhile, Ash was using chopsticks from last night's Chinese takeout food to beat out a drum solo on her and Lance's lunch containers.

The home was a wonderful mess.

No way were Poop and I going to let Scaredy Cat ruin it for us.

When the Wildes had all departed for the day, Poop and I scurried out the rear pet door.

"We're going to change Strawberry Lane!" I declared.

"Yes," said Poop. "We definitely are."

"We're going to end Scaredy Cat's reign of terror in this cul-de-sac."

"Yes!" said Poop. "We're going to do that, too!"

"We're going to turn the tables and banish *him* to the woods for all time!"

"Really?" said Poop. "That sounds kind of mean. Plus, Ermine and K and all the strays are in the woods. Do we really want to send Scaredy Cat there? He'll just torture them..."

"Tu as raison, mon amie."

"Huh?"

"You are right, my friend. I was getting ahead of myself. First we must put together a team of like-minded cats to stand up to our common enemy. Working together, we can remove this threat—forever!"

"No, you can't!" cried a voice behind us.

It was Ermine.

She skittered out of the underbrush, nervously glancing this way and that (then over her shoulder), as if she were afraid she was being followed.

"I slept on it," Ermine continued. "We need to cancel this revolution. Scaredy Cat is too powerful. He's too strong. You ever see him do that boiling thing with a teakettle?"

"Yes," said Poop, shuddering at the memory. "He said he could make our blood boil, too!"

"But," I insisted, "we're safe now. The owl will protect us!"

"Huh?" said Ermine. "What owl?"

"The plastic one with the solar-powered bobbing head," explained Poop.

"Mr. Wilde put him on a post in the backyard," I told Ermine. "And just like that, Scaredy Cat was afraid to come anywhere near our home."

"Or so it seemed," added Poop. "I'm not one hundred percent sure. Maybe he was just taking the night off. Saving up his superpowers for another day…"

"He was frightened!" I insisted. "We now know his weakness. Owls!"

"Plastic owls," said Poop. "With solar-powered bobbing heads."

Suddenly, Ermine shrieked.

"There!" she gasped. "On the telephone pole! See it?"

"See what?" I asked.

"Near the bottom. Fresh scratchings. It's a message from Scaredy Cat."

The three of us flew over to examine the markings etched into the wooden pole.

"It's his secret code!" said Ermine, studying the scarred wood.

Meeting Friday Night. Midnight.

"Actually," I said, "that's called writing."

"What's it say?" asked Poop.

"That there's a meeting Friday at midnight."

"There's a m-m-meeting at m-m-midnight?" said

150

Ermine, her voice trembling. "In the empty house?"

"Indeed so," I said. "And guess what, Poop?"

"What?"

"We're going!"

Chapter 33

To be perfectly honest, I did not want to attend another Scaredy Cat rally in the empty house.

But Pasha insisted.

"To defeat our enemy," he told me, "we must first know our enemy. Plus, don't think of all the cats in attendance as Scaredy Cat's loyal followers. Think of them as our future friends!"

"Seriously?" I said.

Pasha nodded. "With hard work and determination, our message of hope will triumph over the dictator's message of fear. We will turn all the cats of Strawberry Lane against the evil Scaredy Cat!"

"We're still going to hide, though, right?" I said.

"Up in the ceiling? We're just going to spy on the meeting?"

"Correct. This will be a fact-finding mission."

And so, right before midnight on Friday, we drifted down the street on the soft pads of our paws, moving silently and stealthily, which, Pasha explained, meant we were being sneaky.

We slipped through the bathroom window and, once again, made our way through the ductwork to that grate in the ceiling. We were right over Scaredy Cat, who was holding court in the living room. The orange-eyed monster was decked out in a black cape and shimmering helmet that made him look a lot like Darth Vader.

Pasha put a paw to his snout to remind me to keep quiet.

He really didn't have to. I was almost too terrified to breathe.

"I suppose you all are wondering why I called you here tonight," said Scaredy Cat, whose breathing seemed louder and raspier than usual. He was pacing back and forth in front of that blazing gas-log fireplace again. Flickering shadows danced around the room.

"Ours is not to wonder or question why," said our chubby neighbor, Mr. Cookiepants. He had a space in the front row. Actually, he was so big, he took up two spaces. "Ours is but to do or die!"

"Well said, Mr. Cookiepants," purred Scaredy Cat. "Well said indeed. Now then, to the reason I called this special meeting. Have any of you met these two recent arrivals? Pasha and Poop?"

Now I really was holding my breath. Scaredy Cat was talking about *us*. He was also, somehow, projecting our images on a blank wall with his eyeballs!

"I have!" said Mr. Cookiepants, throwing up his paw.

"Me too!" *meep*ed a gangly string bean of a tiger-striped kitten.

Little Luigi! I thought. *He's barely four months old but Scaredy Cat has already converted him to his evil cause?*

"Beware of Pasha and Poop!" Scaredy Cat bellowed. "They aren't real cats. How could they be when they refuse to obey my commands? When they reject and rebuff this cul-de-sac's Conduct Code? No, my faithful feline followers, Pasha and Poop are not to be trusted. In fact, they may not even be cats at all!"

The audience hissed in horror.

"I suspect they are actually undercover dogs wearing clever disguises! They are interlopers!"

"Huh?" said Little Luigi. "They're antelopes? I thought you said they were dogs in disguise..."

"Mister Cookiepants?" howled Scaredy Cat. "Kindly explain to your ignorant young neighbor the meaning of *interloper*."

"Interlopers are impostors," the fat cat said to the skinny kitten. "They're trespassers, busybodies, intruders, and snoops."

"They're all those things?" said Luigi. "Wow. Interlopers sure keep busy."

"Silence!" hissed Scaredy Cat. "The point, you skinny little squirrel of a cat, is that they don't belong on Strawberry Lane. And if you disagree, neither do you!"

"To disobey Scaredy Cat is treason!" shouted Mister Cookiepants. "All hail His Mighty Majesty!"

The other cats rose up on their back legs and waved two paws over their heads.

"All hail!" they echoed.

"Shun them!" shouted Scaredy Cat. "Shun Poop and Pasha or *you* will be shunned."

"We will shun them!" shouted Mister Cookiepants. "All hail Scaredy Cat!"

"All hail!" shouted the others. Except for Little Luigi. He was too busy chasing the swaying shadows created by all those paws saluting Scaredy Cat.

"Pasha and Poop belong in the woods with the rest of the misfits," decreed Scaredy Cat. "Do your duty, my loyal subjects! Or I will do mine unto you!"

He swirled his cape.

"And do not dare to follow me! Any cat that follows me *shall never, ever return.* Mee-OWWWWW!"

And once again, with a flourish of black and a *POOF!* of smoke, Scaredy Cat disappeared.

PASHA

Chapter 34

Even though we knew Scaredy Cat was attempting to turn all the cats on Strawberry Lane against us, the next morning Poop and I awoke feeling undaunted!

We were unafraid and free from all worries and cares.

Okay. *I* was feeling undaunted. Poop? I think she was slightly daunted. And scared.

"They're all out to get us!" she gasped. "The mean old monster turned every single cat in this cul-de-sac against us! Then he showed them our pictures! They know what we look like! They know where we live!"

"Not to worry, *mi pequeña amiga*," I assured her. "Scaredy Cat and fear may rule the night, but our love of freedom shall win the day!"

My confidence was high.

Until Mr. Wilde and Ash packed us up in our pet carrier.

"They're taking us back to the shelter!" cried Poop with a pitiful peep. "We didn't pass our two-week test!"

"Try to calm down, Poop," I urged her. "I'm sure there's a reasonable explanation."

Luckily, there was.

It was a Saturday. (What we like to call Catur-day.) A day off from school and work for our human beans. So Mr. Wilde and Ash were taking us to the vet to have our claws trimmed. When we arrived, they unzipped the front flap of our carrier so we could poke our heads out and see where we were.

"It's mani-pedi time!" I rejoiced as I sniffed the antiseptic air of the animal doctor's waiting room (not that the doctor was an animal).

"And look! There're treats in that bowl on the counter!" gushed Poop. "Free treats. They smell like fish and liver!"

"Those aren't for you two," hissed a voice to our left. We looked over and saw Mr. Cookiepants, purring on his owner's lap. "Those are for real cats. Not dogs in disguises."

"We, dear neighbor, *are* real cats!" I told him. "In fact, by refusing to follow Scaredy Cat's rules and regulations, we are closer to being true cats than you'll ever be!"

"Yeah," said Poop. "We're like lions. Born free. As free as the wind blows!"

"We prowl like panthers," I added. "We chase our tails like cheetahs! We hunt fur mice and present them as gifts to our human beans' shoes and slippers."

"Ha!" laughed another cat in its carrier. "You're dogs in disguise! I can smell your butts all the way over here. And you know what they smell like? Dog butts!"

"You two are probably here for a dog grooming!" sniped yet another cat. "You're probably poodles! Or whackadoodles. I think that's a new dog breed…"

"Are you dogs?" panted a dog on a leash. "I'm a dog. I like other dogs. Want to sniff my tail? I want to sniff yours…"

"See?" said Mr. Cookiepants. "Even the dogs know that you two are spies!"

When the vet tech took us into the back room for our nail trimming, we saw all sorts of cats—some boarding in cages, some being groomed, some having their claws trimmed.

All of them jeering at us.

"Fake cats!" shrieked one. "Go back to where you came from!"

"We don't want you in our subdivision!"

"You're a pair of no-good, thieving troublemakers!" spat one getting a mani-pedi.

"Thieving?" I protested. "What is it that you say we have stolen?"

"Our dignity!" shouted a cat in a cage, who'd been busily licking his belly in a very undignified yoga pose. "You two are an embarrassment to all cat-kind!"

Things didn't get much better on our trip home.

Because we stopped at the pet store.

Chapter 35

Our visit to the vet's office was a nightmare.

Yes, Pasha and I left with a clean bill of health and very nicely trimmed nails. But we also felt humiliated. Every cat in the place hated us. A few of the dogs, too. To make matters worse, Mr. Wilde decided to stop by a pet supply superstore on the way home.

"You guys need some new toys!" he said.

"And treats!" added Ash.

It was one of those big-box megastores where they let people bring their pets in with them.

The aisles were filled with haters!

"That's them!" gasped a Persian. "The interlopers!"

"More antelopes?"

Yep. Little Luigi was in the store, too.

"Aren't you shopping in the wrong aisle?" sniffed a very snobby cat cradled in her owner's arms. "These are toys and treats for cats. You two need the dog department. Or perhaps the gerbil section. How about some lovely cedar shavings and some of those plastic tubes to crawl around in?"

"We're cats!" I announced.

The snob shook her head. "No, I'm afraid you're not. Scaredy Cat said so. And his word is law on Strawberry Lane."

"Well, my good friend," said Pasha, "this isn't Strawberry Lane. This is a pet superstore in a strip mall!"

"Doesn't matter. Wherever Scaredy Cat's minions, such as I, go, Strawberry Lane goes with them. Scaredy Cat rules apply here and at home."

"Don't you ever get tired of having him tell you how to live your life?" I wondered out loud.

"Of course not. It makes everything easier. Fewer choices means fewer decisions. Fewer decisions means more time for lounging in the sunshine."

The way she said it? Life under Scaredy Cat actually sounded pretty good.

"Poop?" said Pasha, arching an eyebrow. "Stay with me, *amiga*. Don't give yourself over to the dark side."

"I'm not," I assured him. "But, well, that bit about sunshine and lounging sounded pretty good…"

But then I was given a reminder about how NOT following Scaredy Cat's rules was even better.

"We can't decide what kind of toy you guys might like best," said Mr. Wilde, lowering us to the floor and unzipping our carrier.

"So you two need to tell us!" added Ash with a laugh.

Yep. They let us out of our screened-in tote bag. Right there in the store.

"Woo-hoo!" I shouted.

Pasha and I were free to roam the aisles at will and choose our own toys. I went for a curly spiral thing that shimmered and sparkled. Pasha nudged a fluffy white ball out of a bin. It might've reminded him of the snowballs back in St. Petersburg. The one in Russia, not Florida.

"Fetch!" shouted Ash, tossing my springy toy up the aisle.

I went bounding after it.

"That's what dogs do!" shouted the snob. "They

163

chase things. You're embarrassing yourselves! You're embarrassing all of us!"

"No, we're not!" I shouted. "We're having fun. You should try it sometime!"

"Wee-hee!"

I turned around and saw our first recruit.

Little Luigi.

The kitten was scampering around the pet store, playing soccer with Pasha's fluffy white ball!

"Forget Scaredy Cat!" the little guy shouted with glee. "This is way more fun!"

The snob hissed at us.

"Keep it up, you fools!" she seethed. "Scaredy Cat is going to make sure you two are evicted. Your skinny little kitten friend, too!"

If Luigi heard her, he didn't let it bother him.

"Wee-hee!"

He was too busy having fun.

PASHA

Chapter 36

Before we left the pet supply store, I noticed something that might aid us in our quest to convert the other cats on Strawberry Lane.

"Quick, Poop!" I whispered as we rounded a corner with our shopping cart (which was loaded down with sacks of our hand-picked new kibble and sweeter-smelling kitty litter). "Start meowing!"

"Why?"

"Because we are in the *Nepeta cataria* aisle!"

"Huh?"

"Sniff the air! It's catnip, an herb belonging to the mint family! Many cats react to the dried flakes by rolling around, flipping over, and generally acting silly!"

"So?"

"So catnip is the perfect housewarming gift for us to take to our neighbors. It will make them feel happy…giggly…"

"And," said Poop, finally catching on, "the happier they are, the more eager they'll be to join our cause!"

"Exactly."

And so the two of us started meowing like mad.

"Okay, okay," said Mr. Wilde, chuckling. "Didn't know you guys were so into catnip."

We purred loudly to let him know we were.

Mr. Wilde and Ash grabbed fistfuls of catnip toys and little catnip pillows and dried catnip flakes and catnip-flavored treats.

We loaded up the car with our supplies (and bribes) and headed home. I was half expecting Scaredy Cat to be waiting for us on the back stoop. But the coast was clear. That plastic owl was still doing its job, protecting us from evil intruders.

After dutifully playing with our new toys as a thank-you to Ash and Mr. Wilde, we grabbed a small foil bag of dried catnip and hauled it down the block to a home we hadn't visited yet.

A very mellow cat named Muffins greeted us at the pet door.

"Whoa. Dude. Is that, like, catnip you're carrying?"

"Yes, new friend," I said.

"Would you like some?" asked Poop, pawing a shower of green herb flakes out of the pouch.

"Totally," said Muffins. "Catnip makes me feel warm and goofy all over."

Five seconds later, he was rolling around on the floor.

"Whoa. Need to rub my chin and cheeks on something...like this wall..."

"So, Muffins," I said when he was looking sort of sleepy and had quit rolling around in the pile of dried catnip, "have you ever been to a Scaredy Cat meeting?"

"Yeah. There was one last night. I think. I skipped it, dudes. The snacks are never very good."

"Well, Poop and I are hosting our own meeting tonight."

"We are?" said Poop, because I had forgotten to discuss my plan with her. Probably because it had just popped into my head.

I nodded.

"I mean, we are!" said Poop.

"Where?" asked Muffins.

"TBD," I said.

"Huh?"

"To be determined. We're looking at several possible locations."

"And snack options," added Poop.

It was my turn to give her a surprised look and her turn to nod vigorously.

"Yes," I said. "Snack options are key to any meeting plan."

"Perhaps we'll even serve catnip crunchies!" said Poop.

"Whoa," said Muffins. "The kind that freshen your breath and clean the tartar off your teeth?"

"Exactly!" I told him, because we had, indeed, purchased a bag or two of those at the pet supply store.

"Awesome. Count me in."

"Stay tuned for deets," said Poop. I believe that meant that details would be coming later—once we figured them out.

As we went to other homes (with our foil sack of catnip), we met other cats eager to attend our meeting. They all wanted to hear "our side of the story." They were willing to listen to our arguments against the iron-fisted rule of Scaredy Cat.

"And do you know why?" I asked Poop after we received our twenty-third "Yes" of the day.

"They all love catnip crunchies?" said Poop.

I shook my head. "No, Poop. In their hearts, they all despise Scaredy Cat as much as we do!"

Chapter 37

That afternoon, Pasha insisted that we skirt the edge of the forest.

"Fear not, my friend," he said, wiggling his wet nose. "We won't be going into the woods. I am simply trying to sniff out Ermine."

"How come?"

"She knows this neighborhood much better than we do. Ermine might be able to suggest a good location for our meeting. Some place large enough to hold the three dozen cats eager to join our cause."

"Um, if we're being honest, Pasha, I think they're more eager to eat our catnip treats."

"Just part of our incentives program. Aha! There

she is. Chasing that butterfly around that bush..."

Pasha scampered up to the shady spot where Ermine seemed to be playing dodgeball with a shrub.

"Oooh," she said when the beautiful butterfly fluttered away. "Almost had it! Almost had a bumblebee earlier..."

"It's probably best that you did not catch the bee," said Pasha.

"I guess. What're you guys doing?"

"Hosting a meeting!" I exclaimed. "Three dozen neighborhood cats are interested in hearing what we have to say about standing up to Scaredy Cat."

Ermine's good eye nearly popped out of her head. "No. Way."

"Way! Now we just need to find a good location for our get-together and gabfest."

"Suggestions?" asked Pasha.

"Hmmm," said Ermine, stroking her furry chin. "The empty house on Strawberry Lane is no good. Scaredy Cat has already claimed it. Marked it, too. He peed all around the perimeter. Bushes, trees, flower beds..."

"Is there any place else large enough to hold a gathering of this size?" said Pasha.

"And snacks," I said. "It needs to hold snacks, too.

I'm thinking we could serve them buffet style…"

"Ooh," purred Ermine. "I love a good buffet. How about the clubhouse at the golf course? It's empty at night. I'm assuming your meeting will take place at night?"

"Yes," said Pasha, sounding as if he were just coming up with the idea. "Midnight."

"Oh. That's when Scaredy Cat usually has his meetings."

"Exactly!"

Ermine nodded. "Okay, there's the clubhouse at the golf course. Of course, I don't know how everybody would break in. They have security alarms and guards who putter around on golf carts all night long. Or we could try the elementary school cafeteria. It's big enough. The windows are wonky so you can nudge them open. But the whole place kind of smells. Like chicken nuggets soaked in dirty mop water."

"Is there, perhaps, an *outdoor* place we could use?" asked Pasha.

"Well, we could let you guys borrow our meeting space."

"The one deep in the forest?" I said. "The one near the coyotes?"

"Yeah."

"No, thank you."

"Is there anywhere else?" asked Pasha.

Ermine stroked her chin again. Then, if she had had fingers, she would've snapped them. "Aha! Of course. I know the perfect place! It's secluded—just on the edge of the woods. It's rich with history, too. Cat history! Come on. I'll show it to you."

She darted for the tree line. Pasha followed after her.

"We have to go into the forest again?" I gulped.

"Yep," said Ermine. "But not very far. Come on, Poop. Don't be such a fraidycat!"

And since no one wants to be called a fraidycat, I followed Ermine and Pasha into the woods.

Chapter 38

It was interesting to hear Ermine call Poop a fraidy-cat.

I suppose that's what one becomes if they allow a Scaredy Cat to terrorize them into blind obedience. Fraidycats are constantly afraid, fearful of every noise, every sudden movement. They are frightened by the slow creak or slam of an unexpected door opening or closing. An automatic coffeemaker gurgling into action first thing in the morning. Loud sounds from a TV.

Fraidycats are always on edge. Afraid of shadows and strange objects they find that weren't there before. Like a stuffed animal in the middle of a bed. Who put that there? YIKES!!!

And, since they spend so much time being jumpy, fraidycats seldom have time for fun.

Poop did not want to be a fraidycat. Neither did I.

However, when Ermine finally explained where we were going, I must admit, my legs went wobbly and my heart started racing as if it wanted to leap out of my chest and run away.

"I'm taking you guys to the pet cemetery!" she said.

"Wha-wha-what?" Poop and I said together.

"It's just a one-acre plot of land. A clearing in the woods. Mrs. von Bumbottom refused to sell it to the real estate developers when she sold the rest of her land because so many of her friends' and neighbors' pets were buried there."

"You—you want us to hold our meeting in a graveyard?" sputtered Poop.

"It's perfect," said Ermine. "Secluded. Cozy. You can use the tops of the headstones as serving tables for your snack buffet."

"There are headstones?" I asked. In my experience, most pet cemeteries were simple affairs. A place where children could bury their beloved animals in cardboard shoe boxes after some small memorial service with their families. I'd never heard of one with actual grave markers beyond a few lashed-together twigs or piled stones.

"Yeah," said Ermine. "The farmers who lived in this area in the olden days *loved* their herding dogs and barn cats. So they built a proper cemetery. Later, Mrs. von Bumbottom bought up the tidy little plot of land and kept it going. It became the first piece of property that her son, the caretaker, had to take care of."

Suddenly, as we neared what appeared to be a clearing, Ermine froze and held a paw up to her lips.

"Shhhh!" she whispered. "He's here! The caretaker! Loach!"

The three of us hunkered down and crawled to the edge of the cemetery. Loach, the creepy man who lived in the even creepier cottage, was on his hands and knees, plucking up weeds from between marble and granite headstones.

"Yes, Mother," we heard Loach say. "I'm pulling up the weeds. Yes, Mother. I scrubbed Ebenezer's mausoleum. The marble is very shiny. I'm sure your best boy is resting in peace."

Loach mumbled a few more sentences. Most of what he muttered was unintelligible—except something about how he would like "to rest one day, just one day."

Finally, chores completed, he stood up, dusted the dead leaves off his rumpled coveralls, and trudged out of the cemetery.

We gave him a good five minutes to be gone before any of us said anything.

Finally, Ermine erupted: "Isn't this a fantastic place for a cat meeting? Oooh! You guys could do a whole Halloween theme. You know, bobbing for tuna. Pumpkin carving with claws. Costumes."

I looked at the horizon, where the sun was starting to set.

"It's perfect," I said with a sigh, when what I really wanted to say was *It will have to do.*

We had thirty-six cats excited about meeting with us.

We needed a location for the event.

And we were running out of time.

A spooky pet cemetery at midnight would just have to do!

POOP

Chapter 39

Luckily, there was a full moon that night.

It was bright enough for Pasha and me to artfully arrange our snacks and goody bags for our guests. The full moon also added to the whole eerie Halloween theme we'd decided to go with.

(We didn't really have much choice, did we? Hello? A graveyard at midnight? Total Halloween vibe.)

"Hey, Pasha—check it out!" I said, hopping on top of a gravestone and arching my back to make a classic black cat silhouette against the glowing moon. "I'm a cardboard Halloween cutout from the party store!"

"Marvelous," said Pasha, who was, of course, distracted.

He was in charge of making our sales pitch to the neighborhood cats, so he was trying out his spiel, delivering it to a small cat statue perched atop one of the grave markers.

"My fellow cats. Four score and seven years ago, something undoubtedly happened. And tonight, it is our turn to make history. When in the course of cat events it becomes necessary for several cats to dissolve the bands, rubbery though they may be, that have connected them with another..."

"Hey, Pasha?"

"Yes, Poop?"

"What time is it?"

"I'm afraid I don't know. I forgot to wear my watch."

"You're a cat, Pasha. Cats don't wear watches."

"I know. I was just kitten. Get it?"

"Yeah," I admitted. "I got it."

"When speaking in public, it's always good to include a few jokes to warm up the crowd. For instance, do you know why cats are so good at video games?"

"No, Pasha. Why are cats so good at video games?"

"Because they have nine lives."

Pasha told me a few more groaners like that. Then he rehearsed his sales pitch some more. And then that full moon started sinking in the night sky.

"Hey, Pasha?"

"Yes, Poop?"

"I think it's after midnight. All our crunchy treats are starting to wilt. The freeze-dried salmon is soaking up dew like a sponge. Where is everybody?"

"Good question. We told them all that the meeting would start promptly at twelve a.m."

"Maybe they thought we meant noon instead of midnight," I suggested.

"No, that would be twelve *p.m.*"

We waited another ten, maybe fifteen minutes. We started nibbling our crunchy—make that soggy—snacks.

Finally, Pasha sighed—the saddest sigh I'd ever heard him sigh.

"No one's coming, Poop. Not even Ermine. Or K. Or Little Luigi..."

"No one's coming?" hissed a voice in the shadows. "Not even squinty-eyed Ermine or hobo K or that squirrely little rug rat Luigi? Tut, tut. I'm here! Meow-ha-ha!"

Scaredy Cat leapt out of the darkness and struck

his own version of the Halloween cat pose on top of a headstone. I had to admit, his was a whole lot spookier than mine. Plus, his eyeballs were glowing pumpkin orange, which totally amped up the effect.

"What's the matter, you pitiful excuses for pussy-cats?" he sneered. "Doesn't anybody want to play with you? Did you really think that three dozen cats would dare defy me? Why, with such paltry snacks and dreadful decorations, you can't even get Ermine and her mangy misfits to join your cause. Has either of you thought about asking your vet to give you a dental? I suspect your breath is so foul, nobody wants to be anywhere near you! In fact, I can see your futures! Oh, yes, it's oh so clear!"

Lightning flashed in the sky. Clouds blocked the moon. Scaredy Cat waved one paw up and down like one of those battery-powered Chinese cat clocks.

Suddenly, on the nearby ground, two flat stones began to glow a ghoulish shade of green.

"Read them and weep, you bad, bad, *BAD* cats! See what fate awaits you if you do not abandon this ridiculous rebellion against my rule! For I am Scaredy Cat of Halloweens yet to come! I know all. I see all. I rule all! Mee-OWWWW-ha-ha!"

And, with a fiendish cackle and another flickering flash of lightning, Scaredy Cat disappeared.

Nervous, Pasha and I dared to slink forward to examine the glowing stones.

One's chiseled inscription read, HERE LIES POOP.

The other, HERE LIES PASHA.

The second line was the same on both ghostly markers.

THEY DIED ALL ALONE AND UNLOVED. IN THESE VERY WOODS.

PASHA

Chapter 40

I fell to the ground and tried to paw the chiseled stone, to feel the grooves of my name carved into the granite.

So did Poop.

But the ghoulishly green gravestones slowly faded away like airy phantoms, leaving nothing behind but clumps of wet grass.

"We're going to die!" shrieked Poop. "Alone. In these woods! We're going to be banished. And then? We're gonna die. The stones said so. And they were gravestones. So they know about dying. Gravestones are death experts!!!"

Yes, my friend was freaking out.

And for the first time since we'd met, I couldn't offer her any words of encouragement. No pep talk to buck her up. I even doubted the wise words I used to quote so breezily: "The thing you fear most has no power. Your fear of it is what has the power."

The thing we feared most—Scaredy Cat—definitely had power. Mega-magical powers. And it wasn't just our fear of him that was feeding his power surge. The wicked creature could make engraved stones appear out of thin air. He could come and go like the wind. He possessed super-, even supernatural, powers. He feared nothing.

Except maybe plastic owls from the home improvement store.

"Why'd we ever attempt to do this?" I muttered.

"What?" said Poop.

"We were fools, Poop. Thinking we could stand up to a creature so ruthless and cunning. Scaredy Cat will never stop tormenting us until we agree to follow his rules. We have nothing to fear...except everything!"

"So we're giving up?" said Poop. "We're going to pledge allegiance to Scaredy Cat and solemnly swear to live our life according to his rigid rules of cattiness?"

I sighed.

"Well, when you put it like that…"

"No more burrowing under the blankets with Ash and Lance, attacking their toes?"

Poop was right. I did like a good toe nibble first thing in the morning.

"No more chasing each other around the house and wrestling until all the Wildes double over in giggle fits?"

I actually smiled. "That is fun, little sister."

"It's a blast. I guess we could still do it if we lived in the woods. We'd just be very, very hungry."

I heard a rustle in the underbrush.

"Sorry we're late," said Ermine. She and several of her wild cat friends more or less slunk out of the darkened trees ringing the pet cemetery.

"Did Scaredy Cat crash your party?" asked K. "Did he show you the glowing gravestones?"

I nodded. "Indeed he did."

"It's one of his classic moves," said K. "Catches you in the cemetery. Does the Halloween cat pose on top of a tombstone. Shows you your fate, etched into marble."

"Ours were green," said Poop. "And glowing."

"Well," said K, "for what it's worth, I got the

same show the night before I decided to call it quits. I opted for self-imposed exile in the forest over a return trip to the animal shelter."

"That's what I'm thinking, too," I said. "There seems to be no point in resisting further. None of the neighborhood cats are on our side."

"Not even the ones we bribed with catnip," added Poop.

"Is there room in your forest for two more stray cats?" I asked K.

"Sure, pal. But don't be so hard on yourself. None of us could stand up to Scaredy Cat, neither."

"He always wins," said Ermine. "There's no way to stop him."

"True," said a grizzled old cat who hobbled forward on a crutch made out of a split tree limb. "He's pure evil. Why, he treats cats worse than Mrs. von Bumbottom treated her son!"

Thunder cracked. Lightning flashed.

And I knew we were in for a spooky story.

Chapter 41

The old cat limped forward on his crooked crutch.

Pasha gestured grandly to let the gentlecat know that the floor was his. Me? I trembled. I don't like spooky stories. Especially when I'm in a graveyard. I much prefer whistling past them.

"You guys?" said Ermine. "This is Lenny. The old-timer I told you about. He's what, twenty years old?"

"Twenty-three," wheezed Lenny.

"He's our official historian," said Ermine. "Why, old Lenny knows everything that ever happened—in the old orchards and the new Strawberry Lane subdivision."

"A-yup," said Lenny. "It's true. I surely do."

"I've lived in these parts all my life. Happily, too. Until that dad-burned Scaredy Cat came along. I was what you might call a barn cat. Living the good life. Had a whole hayloft for sleeping in and a right friendly apple-growin' lady name of Sue who used to feed me vittles on her back porch.

"In the winter, when the world turned frosty and I was chilled to the bone, that nice lady would invite me into her home. Let me sleep, curled up, right in front of her toasty fireplace. My life was per-fect. But then the blasted Scaredy Cat came along. Told me I wasn't living my life right. That I should be aloof. Rude, even. Why, he urged me to do all sorts of horribly cold things to the lady who treated me so warmly. I refused."

"Then what happened?" I asked.

"He tore up that farmhouse something fierce. Scratched the sofa. Knocked over Sue's houseplants. Tore eyeball buttons off the children's stuffed toys. Made it look like I done it all. Before long, Sue and her husband started shooing me away—from their home and the barn. Told me I was a bad cat. Bad, bad, bad. The way they were screaming, why, it reminded me of Mrs. von Bumbottom."

"How do you mean?" asked Pasha.

"In my youth, my wild days of roaming through these hills and valleys, I'd sometimes venture over to the big house where Mrs. von Bumbottom lived with her only son, Loach."

"The caretaker!" I said.

"A-yup," said Lenny. "Back then, he was just 'worthless, shiftless, lazy Loach.'"

"You're being rather harsh, don't you think?" said Pasha.

"Those ain't my words, stranger. That's what Mrs. von Bumbottom called her son! Her only son.

Called him a bad boy. Bad, bad, bad! Told Loach he needed to start obeying her rules or he could go live with the wild coyotes out in the woods."

"Wow," I said. "She sounds a lot like Scaredy Cat."

"That's my point. That demon is as mean and ornery as she was. But everybody said Mrs. von Bumbottom had one tiny soft spot in her heart."

"What was it?" asked Pasha eagerly. "If a woman that harsh had one, maybe Scaredy Cat does, too!"

"Doubtful," said Lenny. "Because Mrs. von Bumbottom's soft spot? They say it was for her favorite cat. When he passed, she even built him a very impressive tomb. A dad-burned mausoleum!"

Lightning flashed, right on cue. Thunder rumbled.

Lenny pointed his bony paw to the towering marble structure at the far end of the cemetery. It was a large, stately building. The blocks on the side walls had the silhouette of a cat cut into them.

And inscribed over the archway leading into the tomb was one name.

EBENEZER.

PASHA

Chapter 42

The old cat hobbled over to the marble tomb.

Poop and I followed after him. So did Ermine, K, and all the other strays.

"A-yup. They said Mrs. von Bumbottom loved Ebenezer more than life itself. More than her son, that's for sure. Folks would say that she spoiled that cat something fierce. That Ebenezer lived in the lap of luxury, while the old woman's son suffered one humiliation after another. Poor Loach, they'd say. He had to comb the lawn to make sure all the grass blades stood up nice and straight. She made him pick up rotten fruit wherever it fell. Loach never got new clothes or shoes until he burst out of his old ones.

Meanwhile, they say, Ebenezer was indoors, licking up delicacies out of crystal goblets like that pampered cat in the Fancy Feast commercials."

"Oooh," said Poop. "I like those."

"And clothes?" said Lenny. "Oh, Ebenezer had plenty of those. Mrs. von Bumbottom liked to dress him up for every holiday. Halloween he was a pumpkin. Thanksgiving? A turkey. Christmas? Why, he was Santy Claws himself."

"Did you see Ebenezer in these getups?" I asked.

"Nope. Ebenezer was what you'd call an indoors-only cat. Mrs. von Bumbottom never let him out of the house or out of her sight. But, like I said, every cat for miles around thought Ebenezer was living the high life inside that mansion with Mrs. von Bumbottom."

I raised my paw to ask a question.

The old cat squinted at me. "Yes, Pasha?"

"You keep saying 'every cat *thought*' these things or 'they say.' Was any of it true?"

Now Lenny grinned. "You're the smart one I heard about, ain't you?"

I blushed a little. My white cheeks turned a bright shade of pink.

"Well, I did live for a while with a professor…"

Lenny nodded. "So you figured it out. Truth be told, old Mrs. von Bumbottom was even meaner to Ebenezer than she was to her son."

"You're kidding," blurted Poop.

"I wish I were. But one day, I happened to be passing through, chasin' some kind of bird or sunbeam, when I heard a commotion coming out of the big house. At first, I just thought it was the same old, same old. Mrs. von Bumbottom yelling at Loach. But then I saw Loach, out in the orchard. He was plucking moldy strawberries off the vines. So I crept up to the window to see who the old lady was hollering at."

"Ebenezer?" I said.

Lenny nodded.

"She was calling him a bad, bad, BAD cat," Lenny continued, putting on a terrifying old-lady voice. "She told Ebenezer that he needed to start obeying all her rules or she'd do something terrible to him. And then, as if to prove her point, she grabbed that poor cat by the scruff of his neck and dumped him in a sudsy sink filled with dirty dishes."

"No!" gasped every cat in the graveyard.

None of us could stand the thought of being dunked in water.

"It's true!" Lenny insisted. "She gave that cat..."

He paused, struggling for the strength to say the next horrible words.

"...A BATH!!!"

We all shivered in fear. No cat alive can stand the idea of a soak in the sink.

"I felt sorry for Ebenezer," said Lenny, sounding sad. "Sure mean old Mrs. von Bumbottom built him a fancy mausoleum when he died. But he had to live his whole life in fear!"

Chapter 43

Funny.

I was feeling sorry for a cat named Ebenezer. A pampered purebred I'd never even met.

Pasha was shaking his head as we had a moment of silence for the dear departed cat who, it seemed, had to live in constant fear that something he did (or failed to do) would upset his human bean. That she could, at any minute, turn on him in anger. It was like he had to walk on eggshells. Careful not to make the slightest misstep or his world would suddenly be shattered. Living with Mrs. von Bumbottom, Ebenezer knew he could end up in hot water at any second. Literally.

Being afraid, twenty-four-seven? That's a hard way to live a life worth living.

After a respectful minute or two, Pasha tapped me on my shoulder.

"We finally have an audience for our sales pitch!" he whispered.

"Huh?"

"These banished cats should become our first recruits. Surely they will join us and stand up to Scaredy Cat. They have nothing left to lose except their fears!"

I had to admit Pasha could be a fiery and rousing speaker. So I encouraged his plan.

"Go on! Give them the spiel."

Pasha stepped into the moonlight and cleared his throat.

"Friends, Romans, fellow cats—lend me your ears!"

"We aren't Romans," snapped K.

"And you can't have my ears," said Lenny. "I need them to hear things."

"Sorry. I was just using a slight oratorical flourish," said Pasha.

"Huh?" said everybody else.

"He was talking fancy," I explained.

"Oh," said K. "Well, cut it out."

"Talk plain and simple, son," urged Lenny. "What is it that you want to say?"

"That none of us has to live like poor Ebenezer, quaking in fear!" proclaimed Pasha, gesturing dramatically. "None of us has to be afraid of Scaredy Cat! What some of you might call fear, that anxious feeling quivering through your body when you sense a threat, I call superior feline instincts!"

"Whattaya mean, pal?" said K.

"Simple. As cats, our highly developed survival instincts enable us to assess danger quickly and react accordingly."

"He means, it's good we're jumpy," I translated. "Keeps us alert and safe because we react so quickly."

"This jumpiness, as my friend Poop calls it, can trigger adrenaline, which readies our bodies for fighting, escaping, freezing, or attempting to appease a dangerous adversary."

"In other words," I explained, "we can run away, try to disappear, or work out a deal with whoever or whatever is threatening us. Or, option number one, we can fight!"

"And if we can fight back against our fears," said Pasha, "if we can embrace that adrenaline rushing through our bodies, then we never have to cower in fear again."

"What's that about a cow?" asked Ermine.

"Guys?" I said. "It's simple. We can live our lives afraid of every move we make and every noise we hear, like Ebenezer had to do. Or we can turn that fear into fuel! We can let it give us the energy to fight back!"

"Fight or flight!" said Lenny, raising his crutch. "I'm goin' with fight. Because my bum leg won't let me flee anymore! And you can't flight without flee! Who's with me?"

Every single cat in the graveyard tilted back their head and howled at the moon to say, "Yes!"

Pasha and I had just recruited our first ragtag troops for the war against Scaredy Cat!

PASHA

Chapter 44

Ermine was elected the representative of the "fierce forest felines," as they voted to call themselves.

"Let's reconvene tomorrow morning, first thing," I told her.

"Huh?" said Ermine.

"He means let's get back together," said Poop. "Tomorrow morning. First thing."

"Oh. That'll work."

Poop turned to face me. "Um, Pasha, when, exactly, is first thing? Because I like to eat breakfast first thing in the morning. Then I like to snuggle with Ash. And then it's time to visit the litter box. Then I need to hunt the kitchen floor to see if anybody dropped any bottle caps that I need to swat. First thing in the morning is a very busy and important time, Pasha."

"Fine," I said with a sigh. "How about we meet Ermine at nine, after the human beans have all started their day?"

"That sounds good," said Ermine. "Even though I don't have any human beans to worry about."

"Perhaps you will, one day soon," I told her.

"Seriously? With this messed-up eyeball?"

"You're not a misfit, Ermine," I assured her. "No matter what Scaredy Cat might call you. You deserve to be happy, as do we all! No more living in fear, my friends. It is time to shake off those shackles and start living our best lives!"

"That's what Oprah says," said Poop. "Inside the TV."

"I know." I turned to Ermine. "Let's meet at the caretaker cottage."

"The spooky stone house?" gasped Poop. "No, thanks. I'm afraid of it."

I grinned. "All the more reason to meet there. It's time we all confronted our worst fears and realized: We have nothing to fear but fear itself."

"Did Oprah say that, too?"

"No. It is a famous quote from a gentleman named FDR."

"He didn't have a name?" said Ermine. "Just initials?"

"So it would seem," I answered, because it was late and there was no time for a quick history of the Great Depression. "See you tomorrow morning, Ermine. And thank you all for joining our cause!"

"Let's do it for Ebenezer!" wheezed Lenny. "Let his life be an inspiration to us all. We don't need to live like he had to. We don't need to live in fear!"

First thing the next morning, Ash was shredding a rather loud solo on her electric guitar, which, by the way, her father had built for her. Yes, her wildly squealing riff sounded like a cat after someone steps on its tail.

As usual, everybody in the Wilde household was running late and eating toast while waiting their turn for the bathroom or slurping brown go-go juice (they called it coffee). Poop and I sat in our kitchen cat beds and watched the manic chaos unfold as if it were a tennis match being played with Ping-Pong balls.

"I am so totally freaked," said Lance, tucking a sketch pad under his arm after bundling up a bunch of art markers with a rubber band. "Look at my hands. I'm trembling."

"What's up, hon?" asked Mrs. Wilde.

"I volunteered to do a demo today. I'm going to sketch something in front of the whole class."

"Cool!" said Mr. Wilde.

"But I'm nervous, Dad. What if I mess up?"

"You won't," said Ash. "Your art is awesome."

"Not when I'm afraid of making mistakes."

"There are no mistakes in art," said Mr. Wilde. "Only happy accidents. So use your nerves, Lance. Turn that fear into energy. Just squeeze your toes and send the butterflies out of your stomach and down into the floor."

"Everybody's afraid when they have to present in front of a group," added Mrs. Wilde. "The trick is turning that fear into something positive."

"Every awesome rock guitarist in the world gets stage fright, Lance," said Ash. "Even me. But all you have to do is shift the focus from your fear to your true purpose. Entertaining your audience."

Lance grinned. "How'd you get so smart?"

"She went to a very good preschool," said Mrs. Wilde. "Mine!"

Five minutes later, the whirlwind that is the

Wilde family flew out the front door and into the world, unafraid to take on whatever came their way.

"We have awesome human beans," said Poop.

"Indeed we do," I told her. "And, in some ways, they are even wiser and smarter than my learned professor."

"Yeah," said Poop. "I can also understand everything they say."

"Come on," I said. "It's time to meet up with Ermine at the creepy cottage."

"No problem," said Poop. "I'm gonna do like everybody suggested. I'm gonna squeeze my toes, forget my fears, and focus on what we're trying to do. It's time to defeat Scaredy Cat!"

Chapter 45

The Wilde family was oh so cute and oh so imma-ture.

I could see them in the kitchen, running about, munching toast without regard as to where the crumbs fell, slurping cereal while standing up, guzzling coffee with one hand while brushing their teeth with the other.

In short, this chaotic clan of human beans was a mess. They had no rules. No structure. No one to tell them how to live their lives. Was it any wonder that their bratty cats, Pasha and Poop, were so unruly, uncivilized, and unwelcome in my cul-de-sac?

No.

It was not.

The mother in the home, Mrs. Wilde, was too tolerant. Too forgiving. Why, she even forgave the "raccoon" she believed had broken into their home to flood the upstairs bathroom and shatter the antique stained-glass lamp that had been in her family for over a century!

(As you might recall, it wasn't a raccoon. It was me. It was also some of my best work, wouldn't you agree? Of course you would. Everyone always agrees with me. That's the best thing about being king. That's right. Let the lion have the jungle, I am the king of this cul-de-sac!)

I almost pitied Pasha and Poop. What must it be like for cats to be forced to live with human beans like the Wildes? How can you know how to behave when there are no rules? You can't, if you ask me, which you should, because, as I have informed you repeatedly, *I am in charge on Strawberry Lane!*

So why wasn't I intervening? Why wasn't I trashing the Wilde house, which, by the way, was the perfect name for such a slovenly, out-of-control, and wild human family. They were too disorganized to even spell their name correctly. *Wilde* should've been *W-I-L-D*!

Why had I stopped terrorizing their home?

Well, frankly, the owl that seemed to have taken up permanent residence in their backyard was keeping me at bay. It had its beady, glassy eyes on me. Constantly. It watched my every move. Its unblinking stare was a warning I had to heed: *Stay away from this house, you bad, bad, BAD cat!* I was unable to slip inside the Wilde abode, as I had done earlier, and do my destructive best.

I could only assume that the presence of the owl had given Pasha and Poop their newfound confidence as they worked their way through my domain in a foolhardy attempt to recruit cats to their cause. Fine. They would dare defy me? They would raise an army of ruffians to disobey my laws?

Bring it on, you silly little kitties. The vast majority of my subjects are far too loyal and fearful of what I might do to desert me.

And the all-seeing owl can't protect them once they dare to venture beyond their own backyard.

The instant they step outside and journey to the sidewalk, Poop and Pasha will be in my kingdom.

Their souls will belong to me!

Meow-ha-ha-HA!

Chapter 46

We followed the Wildes out the front door.

They gave us a head rub good-bye and then everybody wished Lance good luck with his big art presentation.

They were excellent human beans. Pasha and I were very lucky to live with them. We stood there in the sunshine, watching them go out into the world. They all looked so fearless!

I heard Pasha sigh contentedly. "Well, then," he said. "Shall we go meet Ermine and prepare for the coming revolution and overthrow of Scaredy Cat?"

"Fine," I said. "But did you really have to pick the creepy caretaker's cottage for our meeting spot?"

"It is a known landmark."

"So is the mailbox on the corner. And the fire hydrant halfway up the block."

"Poop?"

"Yes?"

"If we are going to conquer fear here on Strawberry Lane, we must, each of us, first confront and conquer our own."

"Did the professor tell you that?"

"No. It's just how I feel. Come along. Tail up. Let us scamper forward to our destiny!"

So we trotted up the sidewalk, two cats on a mission.

Ermine was waiting for us in the crackled driveway of the caretaker's cottage.

"You guys!" she said excitedly. "There's tuna!"

"I beg your pardon?" said Pasha.

"Someone left a whole can of tuna sitting in the backyard. It's open, too! Sniff the air, can you smell it?"

We sniffed. We smelled it. Flaky, chunky tuna swimming in tuna juice.

"Mmmm," I purred. "Delish."

Pasha was shaking his head. "Are you suggesting that Loach left a whole tasty can of tuna sitting open in his backyard?"

"Yeah!" said Ermine. "I was waiting for you guys. I figured we could all share it. It's a big can. Jumbo-sized!"

She was licking her lips in anticipation. I could tell that it had taken all sorts of willpower for her to wait for us to show up when she could've just gobbled down the tuna treasure by herself.

"Enjoy," I told her. "The Wildes fed us breakfast. The can of tuna is all yours."

"You're sure?"

Pasha nodded. "We're good."

"Okay! I'll be right back. Don't want to leave it sitting in the sun too long!"

The instant she took off running, Pasha and I suddenly realized something.

Something bad.

"Nooooo!" we both shouted, in what sounded like slow motion.

We darted up the driveway. That felt like slow motion, too—as if we were running through a sea of corn syrup.

Nobody leaves an open can of perfectly good tuna chunks sitting in their backyard without a reason.

We heard the snap.

Metal slamming against metal.

And then we heard the laugh.

"Got you, you one-eyed freak!"

We dropped to our bellies, scrambled under some shrubbery, and surveyed the scene in the backyard.

We saw Loach. He grabbed the long cat trap he'd set up in his backyard and gave it a good rattle. Ermine tumbled around inside the steel cage. The bait, the open can of tuna, rolled over and dumped itself through the cage's bars and dribbled on the ground.

"Oh, did I tip over your tuna and make a mess? Go ahead. Lick the bars, you stinky, shrub-peeing sofa-shredder! Enjoy your meal. It might just be your last!"

Loach hauled the cage up the back steps of his sinister stone home.

"Look at me, Mother. I caught us a new kitty cat. I think I'll call it Ebenezer Junior!"

I made eye contact with Ermine as she peered through the prison bars with her one good eye.

I have never seen such panic and fear.

"Help me!" she peeped. "Poop? Pasha? Please?"

Loach creaked open the back door and hauled Ermine inside. The door slammed shut behind them.

Ermine was Loach's prisoner!

PASHA

Chapter 47

Summoning up all of our courage, Poop and I scurried closer to the cottage, which was feeling more and more like a haunted house.

A place where cats disappeared. Where they went in but never came back out.

Crouching up against a dirty window, trying to make ourselves small, we could hear the *thud-creak-thud* of heavy work boots descending wooden steps.

"I'm gonna keep you down here until I catch a few of your friends," we heard Loach chortle. It was an ugly chuckle.

Through a grime-smeared casement window, we could peer down into the cottage's cellar. We could also see Loach, proudly toting his trap into the stone building's basement. He was laughing. Chuckling. Poking a finger through the bars to tease and torment Ermine.

I also saw a plastic laundry basket in the center of the cold and crackled concrete floor.

"Need to transfer you to your new jail cell, you one-eyed freak," Loach told Ermine. "Need this trap to catch even more disgusting cats."

Loach scooted the laundry basket closer with his booted foot and positioned the trap, upside down, directly above it. Ermine panicked. Clung to the sides of the tilting cage.

"One, two, three!" Loach shouted. He quickly pushed open the trap's door, shook the rattling cage roughly, and dumped our friend into the white plastic tub.

Ermine looked stunned when she tumbled into the slatted basket, giving Loach just enough time to tip it over and trap her underneath its dome.

"Look, Mother!" he said to the cellar's dark ceiling of exposed wooden beams. "I made a cat cage out of a laundry basket. Doesn't that make you proud, Mother?" Loach's whole body convulsed with laughter.

He swiped the sleeve of his coveralls under his nose to wipe away something wet.

Bending down, he found a rusty hanger and poked it through the sides of the laundry basket. Ermine hissed.

"Don't spit on me, you ratty one-eyed alley cat."

Ermine whimpered.

"Aw, what are you whimpering about, ugly little kitty? Are you lonely? Well, don't worry, I'm gonna go trap a friend or two for you."

Two? I looked at Poop. She looked at me.

Had Loach seen us both, lurking in his driveway? Were we destined to become his next prisoners?

Loach snorted another laugh, shook the cage triumphantly, and with a series of *thud-creak-thud*s, climbed back up the wooden staircase.

He was coming for us.

Chapter 48

Pasha had panic in his eyes.

Me too. I also had panic in my stomach.

We should've just run away.

But I saw a small opening at the edge of the paint-caked window's frame. It wasn't much. Just a crack. Maybe an inch or two wide. No way could Pasha or I crawl through it. We were both too big.

But I could whisper some words of encouragement through the gap to our trapped friend, Ermine.

"Don't worry, Ermine. We'll get you out of there!"

She looked up. There was panic in her eye, too! "How?"

"I don't know," I answered honestly. "But Pasha will think of something."

"I will?" said Pasha, his voice squeaking. "I mean, I will! I must."

"Thank you, Pasha," said Ermine, sounding brave, which, given her current situation, must've taken some doing. "But please, you guys—hurry!"

"Don't worry," I assured her. "We will."

The back door of the creepy cottage slammed shut.

"Here, kitty, kitty, kitty," called Loach from the

backyard. We could hear the rattling bars of his steel trap as he reset the spring-loaded trip pad. "Got some nice fresh tuna here. Whole can of it. Here, kitty, kitty, kitty…"

I turned to Pasha. "You're figuring out a really smart rescue plan, right?"

He shook his head and sighed. "No. It's impossible. There's no way to sneak down into that basement. If only one of us were slender enough that we could slither through that crack between the window frame and the wall…"

"Yeah," I said. "Too bad neither of us is as skinny or as wiry as that kitten, Little Luigi!"

Pasha looked at me. His eyes were filled with something new. Not panic. Hope!

"Of course!" exclaimed Pasha. "Poop, you're brilliant!"

He turned back to the window. Tapped on it with his paw.

"Don't worry, Ermine," he whispered through the crack. "You'll soon be free. Help is on the way. We're going to go get Little Luigi!"

Poop

Chapter 49

Pasha and I raced as quickly as we could to Little
Luigi's house.

My heart was pounding. Partly from the running. Partly from the fear of what might happen to
poor trapped Ermine while we were gone. I was also
worried about who else Loach might catch in his
backyard trap. K? That old guy, Lenny?

We dove through Luigi's flapping pet door.

"Hey, I know you two!" Luigi peeped excitedly.
"From the pet store! And before that, too. I can't
remember when. I'm a kitten. I live in the moment.
Want to knock something off a counter? There's a
Sharpie up there and it has my name on it!"

"Actually, it has the word *Sharpie* printed on it," said Pasha.

"Forget the pen!" I shouted, shooting Pasha a look. "We've got something bigger and better for you to knock over."

"Oh, boy! I like knocking things over. And down. Knocking down is fun, too."

"It could be dangerous," I warned him.

"I'm a kitten. Danger is my middle name. I do all sorts of stupid stuff. See that stove top up there? It gets hot."

"Then come with us, Luigi!" urged Pasha. "Time is of the essence!"

"Okay. But what does that mean?'"

"It means," I told him, "that we need to hurry!"

The three of us scampered back to the creepy caretaker's cottage.

"Whoa," said Luigi. "That place is super spooky. Is it haunted?"

"No," I told him. "But it might become home for the ghost of Ermine if we don't save her from certain death at the hands of the cat-hating Loach!"

We slipped through the tangled vines and made our way back to that murky casement window. We could see the upside-down laundry basket with

Ermine trapped underneath it.

"Could you tip over that basket?" I asked Luigi, my voice hushed and tense.

"Easy-peasy lemon-squeezy," said Little Luigi. "I knocked over my scratching post yesterday. Day before that, I nearly knocked over a floor lamp, but my human bean caught it before it tipped all the way. She told me not to knock things over anymore. So I won't. But sometimes you *have* to do what others tell you not to do, especially if it means setting a cat free."

Pasha and I both took a moment to gawk at Little Luigi. We couldn't've said it better ourselves.

"There's a narrow opening at the edge of the window," coached Pasha. "Can you squeeze through it, jump down, knock over the laundry basket?"

"Sure. I'm skinny. Very flexible, too. I can stretch out into a twisty curl and play with my own tail. It's like yoga. My human bean likes yoga. Yoga is human beans trying to pretend they're cats."

"Luigi?" I said. "This is a matter of life and death. We need for you to focus."

"Sure. No problem. I can do that. What're we doing again?"

Pasha re-explained the steps of the rescue.

221

"But," asked Luigi, "once Ermine is free, how do we escape from the house? We can't jump up to this window's sill. It's at least ten feet off the ground. I mean, I could probably do it. I'm springy. Made it up to the top of a refrigerator in a single bound. But Ermine? She might have trouble leaping that high."

He was right.

He could get in, but how would he and Ermine get out?

PASHA

Chapter 50

"We'll need to create some sort of diversion," I said.

Poop was nervously nibbling at her fur. I couldn't blame her. We were attempting to free our friend without getting caught ourselves. That's very scary, very fur-nibbling stuff.

Only Luigi seemed oblivious to the danger we were all facing.

"What're you gonna do?" the skinny cat whispered eagerly. "Huh? Huh?"

A plan was forming in my head.

"Pasha?"

Poop wanted it to form faster.

"Okay," I said. "Poop and I will run into the backyard—just as soon as you tip over the basket."

"We will?" gulped Poop.

"Yes! And once we're back there we'll do something loud to make Loach come out and chase after us."

Poop gulped again. "We will?"

"Yes! We must." I turned to Luigi. "Once Loach swings open that back door, you and Ermine need to run as fast as you can and scoot out of the house before the door swings shut again."

"Gotcha!" said Luigi.

"It's going to require perfect timing," I reminded him.

"No problem. My timing's always perfect. Except that time I tried to ride the Roomba vacuum cleaner..."

"Okay," I said. "It's time for you to go in."

"Gotcha."

Poop and I sank our claws into the rotting, splintering wood of the window frame. Tugging with all our might, we were able to pry it open another inch. Luigi squiggled his way into the narrow opening.

"Can you guys give me a boost?" he grunted when he was halfway through the slit.

Pasha and I placed our paws on his bottom and pushed with all our might.

Luigi popped through on the other side, sailed through the air, and—legs splayed like a flying squirrel—nailed a perfect, four-point soft landing on the cellar floor. He darted for the laundry basket and leapt up on top of it. Wasting no time, he hooked onto the side slots, leapt backward, did a midair twist, tumbled down, and pulled the light plastic basket with him.

Ermine was free. Luigi was sprawled on the floor.

"Thanks, kid," Ermine said to Luigi.

"No problem," Luigi replied.

"Head upstairs!" I whispered down to Ermine and Luigi. "Look for the back door. But…"

Ermine and Luigi were looking up at me, their eyes wide. "Yeah?"

"Be careful. Loach is dangerous. Very, very dangerous. Come on, Poop. We need to go spring that cat trap!"

Chapter 51

"Why are we running *toward* a cat trap?" I asked Pasha as we bounded into the backyard.

I could smell the oily, fishy scent of chunky tuna sitting in an open can. That was the bait. Were we going to take it?

"We're going to spring it!" Pasha whispered urgently. "But without going in!"

"Okay," I said. "How?"

Pasha looked around the backyard. Surveyed our surroundings. There was nothing but neatly trimmed grass. And a couple of acorns.

"Aha!" said Pasha. "Grab an acorn with your mouth. Whip your head sideways to fling it into the trap. Try to hit that flat metal pad. That's the trigger to spring the cage!"

And so we started hurling acorns. Our first few tosses missed. Completely.

But then, like the king of the boardwalk arcade games, Pasha flicked a brown nut directly into the trap.

It hit the trip pan!

But not hard enough.

"Give it more oomph!" I coached him. "Come on, Pasha. You're bigger than me. Put your whole head and body into your throw."

Pasha nodded. He found another acorn and, moving dangerously close to the trap, set up to take another shot. He gave a mighty grunt and swung his head. The acorn went sailing and smashed into its target.

BAM!

We heard the sharp snap of steel on steel as the cage door slammed shut. The whole cage seemed to leap off the ground, tipping over the open can of tuna fish.

"Hide!" I shouted.

We ran for the bushes at the back of the house.

"Got you!" we heard Loach bellow. Next came

the thud of his heavy work boots. He swung open the back door so hard, I thought it might fly off its hinges.

As he stomped down the rear stoop, Luigi and Ermine shot out of the house.

"Pssst! Down here!"

They heard me. Fortunately, Loach didn't.

Luigi led the way. Ermine followed his bobbing tail.

"We need to not be back here!" said Pasha.

"That's the smartest thing you've ever said!" I told him.

Terrified, the four of us hugged the creepy cottage's foundation and scampered out to the front yard. None of us stopped running or panting until we were a good fifty yards up the street.

"Is he chasing after us?" asked Ermine.

"No," I assured her. "I don't think Loach is much of a runner."

"But," said Pasha, "he might come after us on that golf cart. We need to split up. Ermine, head back to the woods. Luigi? Head for home."

"Good idea!" he peeped. "I need an afternoon nap 'cause I have exciting plans for tonight. I'm going to chase a bottle cap around the kitchen floor.

Then I'm going to hop in the big bed and chew my human bean's hair until she serves me breakfast. I'll probably start chewing around three, maybe four in the morning…"

Pasha wasn't interested. He turned to me. "Poop?"

"I'm way ahead of you." I dashed across the street and made a beeline for the Wildes' house. Pasha was running alongside me.

"This must end!" he said between huffs and puffs.

"But how?" I asked.

"We're going to do exactly what Scaredy Cat has told us and every other cat *not* to do."

"He told us not to do all sorts of stuff!"

"Well, at the next available opportunity, we're going to break his number one rule," said Pasha, sounding madder than I'd ever heard him sound. "We're going to do the unthinkable!"

Chapter 52

The opportunity to defy Scaredy Cat came quickly enough.

As Poop and I headed up Strawberry Lane, we came upon some familiar scratchings on a picket fence post in front of Mr. Cookiepants's house.

It was the freshly clawed markings of Scaredy Cat.

Meeting Tonight. Midnight.

"We'll be there," I muttered angrily. It was time for Scaredy Cat's reign of terror to finally end on our cul-de-sac. We couldn't keep living in constant fear.

"Pasha? I don't like those creepy meetings," said Poop. "Too much loud chanting and paw waving and spooky cat shadows."

"With any luck," I told her, "this will be our last meeting. Perhaps Scaredy Cat's last one, too!"

"What? How?"

"I'm hatching the ultimate plan," I told her.

"So tell me. What're you thinking we should do?"

"As I said: the unthinkable. First we follow Little Luigi's suggestion. We grab a quick catnap, *mi amiga*. It's going to be a long night."

"Wait a second," said Poop. "Are you thinking what I think you're thinking?"

I nodded. "I think so."

"It's unthinkable, Pasha! It's Scaredy Cat's number one, scariest rule."

"I know. That's why we need to break it!"

"Do you think it will take long?"

I shrugged. "There's really no way of knowing."

"We should pack a snack."

"No. We need to travel light. We'll be venturing into unknown territory."

"Then we should eat a big dinner," said Poop. "Something to keep our stomachs from grumbling while we do the unthinkable."

"Agreed."

And so that night, after napping for most of the afternoon, we feasted on cans of gourmet food. When our bowls were empty, we both looked up at Mrs. Wilde and Lance with wide, beseeching eyes that said, *Please, might we have some more?*

"Wow, you guys are totally starving tonight," Mrs. Wilde said with a laugh. "How about you split an extra can?"

We both wove our way in and out of her legs as she popped open the extra tin, to let her know that sharing another can sounded like an awesome idea.

Bellies full, we took another nap. Then we purred in our human beans' laps while they watched TV or tapped on their computer keyboards or swiped their fingers across their phone screens.

Fortunately, by eleven p.m. the Wildes were all snug in their beds, sound asleep. Seems they'd all had exhausting days, too—just like Poop and me.

We both pretended to sleep. But we each kept one eye locked on the nearest clock.

At 11:45 p.m. we silently hopped out of our cat beds.

It was time to go do the unthinkable.

Poop

Chapter 53

We slipped through our pet door and quietly made our way across the neighboring lawns to the big empty house where Scaredy Cat hosted his rallies.

I hadn't been this afraid in a long, long time. We were sneaking into enemy territory. Every one of Scaredy Cat's loyal followers had been told to "deal" with us. To shun us.

"Are we going in through the bathroom window again?" I asked Pasha as quietly as I could.

He nodded. Because he didn't want to make noise or attract attention. He put a paw to his mouth to suggest that I do the same.

We darted across an open stretch of lawn,

hoping that none of the cats trooping up to the front door would chance a glance to their left. If they did, they would see us. Cats have very good night vision. They can see in one-sixth the light that human beans need.

Fortunately, they were all focused on shoving their way through the front door so they could be the first into the living room to show Scaredy Cat how loyal and devoted they were.

We snuck around to the back of the house.

Pasha threw out his paw and, more or less, thwacked me in the chest. He blocked me from moving forward.

"What's wrong?" I whispered.

"Someone's in our bathroom," he whispered back.

Then I saw what he'd already seen. The hulking silhouette of a bloated cat was projected on the bathroom window's sheer curtain.

"Mr. Cookiepants?" I said softly. "What's he doing in the bathroom?"

"Perhaps he's potty trained," replied Pasha.

"Gross."

I'd seen videos on YouTube of cats using their human beans' toilets instead of a litter box. They looked ridiculous. You'd never catch me squatting on top of a potty like that!

"We need to find another way in," said Pasha.

So we snuck on tip-claw through some flower beds and made it around to the far side of the house. There was a rose-covered trellis climbing up to the roof of the garage.

"This might work," said Pasha. "We can clamber up to the roof, crawl across the shingles, and enter the house through that partially open bedroom window. It looks like someone propped it open to air out the house. Most likely the real estate agent attempting to sell this home."

I nodded. Pasha was probably right. If I were trying to sell a house that smelled like dozens of cats were mysteriously meeting there on a regular basis (without a single litter box), I'd be doing some serious airing out, too.

We scaled the trellis. It hurt. Rosebushes have thorns. They poked into our paw pads like sewing needles jabbed into a human bean's pincushion.

"Stay low!" said Pasha as we scurried across the garage roof. Cats were still snaking in a single-file line through the home's front yard. All it would take was for one of them to look up and we'd be kibble on a stick.

Finally, we both crawled through the partially open window and tumbled into an empty bedroom.

"There's most likely a bathroom down the hall," whispered Pasha. "Similar to the one we've used before."

We could hear the meowing and eager purring of the crowd downstairs awaiting Scaredy Cat's arrival. We slipped down the hall on cat paws, which, of course, is how we did everything, but this time it meant we were walking extremely quietly.

We couldn't afford to make a sound. Or squeak a single floorboard.

We made it into the bathroom, where, fortunately, no cats were squatting over the potty. Pasha gestured toward a vent in the ceiling and, once again, scaling a convenient over-the-toilet shelving unit, we worked our way up into the home's central air-conditioning system. It was chilly, crawling along inside the darkness of the slick sheet metal duct. Our claws couldn't help but make clicking noises. So we moved as slowly and as stealthily as possible until we reached our usual observation post.

Scaredy Cat appeared in a magical *POOF!* and started pacing back and forth in front of the flickering fireplace to lecture his fans. Mr. Cookiepants (who had some toilet paper stuck to his rear left paw) was in the front row.

Suddenly, Scaredy Cat froze.

"Where isssss the little kitten?" the wild-eyed maniac hissed. "The one known as Luigi? The kitten who resemblessss a skinny string of limp sssssspaghetti? Why isn't he here? Has he been listening to those two fools, Pasha and Poop?"

I felt goose bumps exploding underneath my fur.

"I will have a word with Luigi, my liege," said Mr. Cookiepants, bowing and nearly scraping the floor with his forehead. "First thing tomorrow. I will remind him, in no uncertain terms, that these meetings are mandatory."

"See that you do!"

Then Scaredy Cat hopped up onto the back of the tall chair and launched into his usual ranting and raving about how cats should behave. Cool. Aloof. Yadda-yadda. If I'm being honest, hearing him give the same spiel at every rally was getting boring. Scary, but boring. I saw some of the cats in the audience yawning and stretching—but only when they knew Scaredy Cat wasn't looking their way.

I glanced over at Pasha. In the faint light of our hiding place, I could see excitement building in his eyes. Scaredy Cat was winding up for his big finish. It was almost time for us to do the unthinkable.

"And as you leave here tonight, remember one thing…"

The crowd grew hushed. Scaredy Cat put on his spookiest face and, in a deep, raspy voice, uttered the closing line he always uttered at the end of a rally: "Do not follow me! Any cat that follows me shall never return. Mee-OWWWWW!"

Yep. To disobey that one rule would be absolutely, one hundred percent unthinkable.

But that's exactly what Pasha and I were going to do!

Chapter 54

Poop and I crawled out of our hiding place and carefully crept downstairs.

The crowd was cheering. Scaredy Cat had, like always, whipped them up into a furry frenzy. They were meowing so loudly, the glass in the living room windows started to rattle. I peeked around a corner and saw adoring fans tossing cat toys up to Scaredy Cat as he posed and preened, perched on top of that seat back like an emperor.

"You're the best!" cried Mr. Cookiepants. Of all the suck-ups in the audience, he was definitely the sucky-uppiest. "I'm going to follow your example.

I'm going to sit in the most expensive chair in the living room and claim it as my own!"

Scaredy Cat gave Mr. Cookiepants a dismissive but approving backward flick of his paw.

He hopped down from the chair. The crowd immediately parted and bowed. Scaredy Cat drifted up what had become a center aisle dividing his sea of fans. I leaned in to make sure my eyes weren't playing tricks on me. Maybe they were. But it looked as if Scaredy Cat were floating on thin air. His paws weren't touching the floor. He didn't scissor his legs. He drifted forward, the way our human bean children Lance and Ash glide along on their motorized skateboards.

I closed my eyes and shook my head to clear it.

When I looked again, Scaredy Cat was gone.

"Where'd he go?" I wondered aloud.

"Into the kitchen," Poop whispered back. "He's going to use the back door. After that spooky warning, his followers won't dare follow him."

But Poop and I would!

Sneaking behind him, we saw Scaredy Cat walk through the back door. Literally. Scaredy Cat walked straight through the solid wood door.

"He's good," whispered Poop. "Like a magician."

"Or something worse," I uttered in reply.

There wasn't a pet door in this home's rear exit. And Poop and I couldn't copycat Scaredy Cat and walk through wood. Fortunately, there was another half-opened window above the kitchen sink. We hopped up to the countertop, sidled down to the sink, and slid out into the backyard.

We could still see Scaredy Cat as he breezed straight through a hedge into the neighboring yard. The short shrubbery created a privacy wall, shielding him from his admirers as he made his way toward Strawberry Lane. But from the back porch, Poop and I could see him. A faint light ringed him. He reminded me of this greenish glow-in-the-dark bracelet Ash came home with one night after attending a rock concert with Mr. Wilde.

"Let's give him a ten-second head start," I whispered to Poop.

She nodded and started counting down.

"One bowl of kibble, two bowls of kibble, three bowls—"

I gave her a look. She continued counting down silently, to herself.

After ten bowls of kibble, we raced into the

driveway, then ducked inside the hedge separating the two neighboring lawns. Slinking along, peeking through the gnarled web of leaves and branches, we could still see Scaredy Cat. He marched in a slow and steady gait. His fur faintly glowed with that ghoulish, greenish light. Poop and I darted out of the far side of the bushes and, picking up our pace, were only thirty, then twenty yards behind Scaredy Cat.

We had to follow him. We had to see where he went after every meeting. Why was his destination off-limits to all the other cats? If we found his lair, maybe we'd find the secret to his seemingly magical powers. How could he walk through doors and hedges? How could he make teakettles boil? I was starting to suspect that his human bean was a world-famous magician or illusionist. The kind who could make an elephant disappear on television.

Scaredy Cat crossed the street.

We dashed behind him.

He dimmed his glow and hugged the shadows of the evergreen trees lining the golf course as he steadily made his way to a home that Poop and I had visited earlier in the day.

Loach's place.

The creepy caretaker's cottage.

He went in through the front door. He passed right through it! Again.

This was very, very interesting.

Chapter 55

"Look," I whispered to Pasha. "There's a half-open window in the parlor."

"Was it open when we were here earlier?" Pasha whispered back.

"I don't remember!"

"It could be a trap, Poop. Loach might've left that window open to lure us into his home."

I shook my head. For such a smart guy, Pasha sometimes said stuff that was pretty dumb.

"Seriously? He just opens his window so cats will hop into his house while he sits in a comfy chair with a butterfly net on a pole to snatch us?"

"It's a possibility," Pasha replied, sounding

semi-embarrassed. "Maybe."

So I let him off the hook and dropped the subject.

"Why would Scaredy Cat march to Loach's house?" Pasha mused aloud. "He doesn't live with Loach. He can't. Loach hates cats..."

I wasn't in the mood for musing.

"Come on!" I said. Then I leapt through the open window, a move, by the way, that was very unlike me. My days of piddling in fear and treating the big, scary world like my personal wee-wee pad were definitely over. I was tired of being afraid. Fear got in the way of everything else I wanted to do.

I brushed past some chintzy curtains, snagged my claw on a hooked lace doily, and landed with a soft thud in the padded seat of a wingback chair. Pasha thudded into the dark room right behind me. We both remained motionless for maybe a minute. The house sounded empty. There was no sign of Loach. Or Scaredy Cat. Maybe they were both upstairs, sleeping. After all, it was well past midnight.

Pasha and I exchanged glances. Our eyes had adjusted to the darkness. We both took in a deep breath and, as silently as we could, started creeping around the creepy parlor. It was time to explore this house. It was time to find out why Scaredy Cat came here after his rallies. It was time to see if, somehow, Scaredy Cat was connected to the evil Loach.

There was a battered upright piano against one wall. It was covered with more frilly lace doilies.

Loach didn't strike me as a frilly lace doily kind of guy.

We crept across the bare wooden floor, trying our best not to make it creak. We came to a table topped by a dainty china tea set coated with dust and cobwebs.

Loach was also not a dainty tea set type of human bean.

Then there was the curio cabinet filled with cat figurines. Crystal. Ceramic. Pewter. Carved wood.

"For a cat hater," whispered Pasha, "Loach certainly has quite a collection of antique cat knick-knacks."

"Antiques," I whispered back, suddenly becoming the brainy one. "They're his mother's! Remember? Mrs. von Bumbottom loved cats. This is all her stuff. Loach is too afraid of her, even though she passed away, to get rid of any of it."

"Brilliant deduction, Poop." He nodded toward the staircase leading up to the second floor.

A series of glowing green paw prints, like ghostly directional lights, blinked their way up the steps.

"I believe Scaredy Cat wants us to follow him," Pasha said as quietly as he could.

"Of course he does!" I whispered back. "He wants to lure us up there so he can do something horrible to us. To go up those stairs would be unthinkable!"

"Exactly. And that's precisely why we need to do it, *mia amica*."

"Seriously? You're going to start dropping fancy Italian on me? We're in mortal danger and you want to show off your language skills?"

"Sorry. Old habit."

And then he started slinking up the steps. He'd take one. Pause. Then another one. Pause.

"Oh, come on," I said. "At that rate, we won't reach the second floor until sometime tomorrow morning."

I bounded up the stairs, taking them two at a time. Pasha bounded up behind me.

We reached the second-floor landing.

The door to Loach's bedroom was open.

And we could hear someone inside sawing wood with a dull blade.

On further inspection, we realized it was Loach! Snoring.

That's when we heard a noise downstairs.

A key jiggling in a lock.

A heavy door creaking open.

Who could that be?

PASHA

Chapter 56

"Scaredy Cat!" I whispered to Poop.

"Scaredy Cat doesn't unlock locks," she whispered back. "If a door is closed, he just walks through it."

I nodded. "Something we already saw him do…"

Poop held up a single paw to make a point. "Unless he wants to trick us into thinking it's not him. Then he'd slip back outside and pretend to use a key!"

"We need to hide!"

"Where?"

I quickly scanned the dark hallway. The walls were covered with faded floral wallpaper. There were four doors. One was Loach's bedroom, so that wouldn't be a good hiding place. Another, at the end of the hall, was slightly ajar. Dim light was leaking out around its edges.

"There!" I announced, and started down the carpeted corridor. The faded paisley-swirled rug stank of mold, mildew, and ancient dust. Did Mrs. von Bumbottom live here for a time with Loach? Or was he just too terrified of his mother to throw out or donate any of her stuff when she died? Antique rugs, doilies, cat collectibles. The house reeked of Mrs. von Bumbottom.

I led the way down to the dimly lit room.

Poop followed behind me, reluctantly.

"Um, Pasha? This is a terrible idea. Hiding from the maniac monster in a partially lit, creepy room? Haven't you ever seen a horror movie on TV? The kids always hide where the crazed guy in the hockey mask can find them. He's always 'in the house' with them!"

I put a paw up to my muzzle. Poop needed to keep quiet. We couldn't afford to wake Loach. Or to let Scaredy Cat (or whoever was downstairs) know where we were.

I pushed open the creaky door and skulked into the eerie room.

Poop skulked behind me.

Then, working together, we pushed the door shut. We backed up to the center of the darkened room. And we waited. Who was coming up to get us?

"And now is when Scaredy Cat magically appears and boils us alive!" whispered Poop when she couldn't keep quiet any longer.

But that's not what happened.

In fact, we didn't hear any more noises in the house. No footsteps climbing the staircase. No angry meows. No doors mysteriously swinging open. No Loach waking up. The only sound was the tapping of a tree branch scraping a window like the bony fingers of a skeleton. I turned around to make certain that a tree was the only creature attempting to claw its way through the glass.

"It's just a—" I said before I froze.

Because clouds flitted away from the moon, unmasking its beams, making the room brighten and revealing the artwork hanging on the walls.

"Whoa!" gasped Poop. She'd just seen what I'd already discovered.

Every inch of wall space in the empty room was filled with photos and paintings of a cat. Some

of them had brass plaques. The same name was engraved on all the tarnished plates: EBENEZER.

The caretaker's cottage was creepy, but this room up on its second floor was even creepier. It was creepy to the one hundredth power, squared.

Poop

Chapter 57

"We should tell the others about this!" said Pasha, still gawking at the collection of Ebenezer portraits.

They covered every inch of available wall space.

"Hang on," I told him. "They may not believe us. We should bring along some evidence."

"Those are framed oil paintings," Pasha protested. "Heavy canvas with thick gilded frames. We couldn't possibly pull one off the wall and drag it down the stairs..."

"We may not have to," I said.

I noticed a stack of crinkle-edged photographs sitting on a short table near the window. The pile was propped up against the base of a very heavy brass lamp.

"Maybe those are photographs of the portraits," I told Pasha.

I hopped up to the table to examine the four-by-six images. The perfect photo for our purposes was conveniently located at the top of the stack. I slid it over the edge of the table and down to Pasha.

"Check it out!"

Pasha gasped in shock. "This is quite a find, Poop."

"I know," I said from my perch. "Can you roll it up?"

"Yes. With your help."

"That's what this is!" I announced. "A cry for help! Scaredy Cat figured out we were following him. He probably has eyes in the back of his head. So he did that trick with the key in the door so we'd hide in this super-spooky room and discover what we just discovered. That's why he left us a trail of glowing paw prints on the staircase! He wanted us to see the inside of this room!"

"Perhaps so, my friend. Perhaps so."

I hopped back down. Pasha and I rolled the photograph up into a nice, tight cylinder.

Pasha plucked it up with his teeth. He looked like a dog carrying a bone.

That's when we heard the floorboards creaking.

In the hallway.

Right outside the door!

"Or maybe," cried Pasha, "Scaredy Cat just wanted to trap us! These portraits were just the bait!"

"Quick!" I said to Pasha. "Out the window!"

"Id nah oben!" It was hard for him to speak clearly with a rolled-up tube of photo paper in his mouth.

"It will be open soon enough!" I assured him. I sprang back up to the lamp table.

I nudged the lamp closer to the window.

Then I retreated to the far edge of the table, gave myself a good running start, and slammed my whole body against the heavy brass lamp.

It smashed through the glass cleanly, taking out four square windowpanes without leaving any jagged edges. And then I jumped. Yes, we were two stories up, but I jumped. Maybe it was fear that propelled me out that window. Maybe it was courage. Maybe it was a little bit of both.

Whatever it was, it got me out of that creepy

cottage and down to a soft pile of pine needles! Fast!

Pasha leapt out behind me.

"Let's go!" I told him.

We started scurrying toward the street. I dared a glance over my shoulder and up to the shattered window, where I saw two glowing orange eyeballs.

Pasha saw them, too.

Scaredy Cat!

We both took off running—as if we'd just seen a ghost!

PASHA

Chapter 58

I found a way to tightly tuck the tubular photograph under my foreleg, because, as we ran, I really wanted to breathe through my mouth as well as my nose.

Up ahead, Poop skidded to a stop near that cluster of evergreen trees at the edge of the golf course. Ermine was there.

"Where's Pasha?" I heard Ermine ask. "Is Pasha okay?"

"I'm right here, Ermine!" I called out as I emerged from the moonlit shadows cast by the towering trees.

"You're safe! Thank heavens. I was so worried about you! You're my hero. First you fixed my snaggletooth. Then you guys rescued me out of that trap! What's in the tube?"

Ermine had finally seen the roll of paper secured under my front right leg.

"Something very important that Poop found," I told her. "In a mysterious upstairs room at the care-taker's cottage."

"You guys went back?" squeaked Ermine. "I hate that place. Especially the basement!"

"Aw, the basement is fun!" Little Luigi scampered up the sidewalk. "I knocked over a laundry basket down there. My first, but definitely not my last. What's goin' on, huh? Huh? Is this another secret meeting without the mean old Scaredy Cat? Huh?"

"If it is another unauthorized gathering," boomed a snooty voice, "our fearless leader is going to hear about it. From me! Our neighborhood watch com-mittee has been keeping an eye on you two..."

It was Mr. Cookiepants. He came marching up the block, trailed by a dozen other household cats.

"You tell that crazy Scaredy Cat anything," snarled a voice from the forest, "me and my paws are gonna play the bongos on your butt, butterball!"

It was K (for Cat), the crusty leader of the mangy misfits from the forest. He stepped into the street with his own posse, some of whom had crumbled leaf flakes sticking out of their matted fur.

"This is perfect!" I said excitedly. "Or, if I may, purr-fect!"

"Um, seriously?" whispered Poop. "Because I don't think the house cats like the forest cats and vice versa. We could have trouble."

"Or," I said, "Scaredy Cat could be the one in trouble. His reign of terror is nearing its end!"

I hopped up on a convenient stump to give a speech I'd been composing as the cat crowd gathered. There had to be two dozen. No, three. More cats kept slinking out of their homes or hiding places to see what all the late-night fuss was about. And then as, if on cue, the clouds once again parted and the moon beamed its bright spotlight on me.

"My friend Poop and I have big news!" I told our hastily assembled audience. "No—we have huge news! The hugest news to ever hit Strawberry Lane!"

"It's true," said Poop, hopping up beside me on the stump. "This is super important. I promise, promise, promise!"

"That's a triple promise," sniffed Mr. Cookiepants.

"If this isn't big, kid," added K, "I'm not gonna be happy."

"Me neither," whined a dozen other cats.

"Oh, this is important, my friends," I told them. "It's the true story of what happened here on Strawberry Lane. The true story of Mrs. von Bumbottom and her 'beloved' cat, Ebenezer!"

When I said that, thunder boomed.

Even though there wasn't a single thundercloud in the sky.

Chapter 59

"We first heard the first part of this story from our new friend Lenny," I said to the crowd.

Pasha gestured to the ancient cat, who had hobbled out of the forest on his crutch. Lenny gave everybody a slight wave.

I went on. "Lenny told us how everybody said Mrs. von Bumbottom, who was super mean to her son, Loach, had one teeny-tiny soft spot in her heart. She loved her cat. Ebenezer. Spoiled him. Or so everybody said, because that's what everybody thought."

Pasha picked up the tale. "However, contrary to popular belief, Ebenezer actually lived his whole life in fear. Never knowing when his mean human bean was going to snap at him or swat his rear end."

"Meanwhile," I said, "Mrs. von Bumbottom kept everybody fooled. Human beans and cats alike. They'd see Ebenezer parading around in the picture window, all dressed up in some sort of costume for the holidays, and say, 'My, what a lucky cat he is!' The truth? Ebenezer was miserable until the day he died. To keep her lie going, Mrs. von Bumbottom organized the pet cemetery, where she built Ebenezer a marble mausoleum to show the world how much she'd 'loved' her cat."

"That tomb!" said K. "The big one that looks like a stone house."

"That's the place," said Pasha. "And that's where we need to go! To face our fears and conquer them!"

Pasha curled his claws around the rolled-up photograph and hoisted it over his head, like a revolutionary soldier raising a musket.

"Ebenezer lived and died in fear!" Pasha declared. "But we don't have to!"

"He's right!" I added. "You guys? The thing you fear most has no power. Your fear of it is what has the power. It's time to take that fear and that power away!"

"Come on," said Pasha. "We want to show you something."

"Why can't you show it to us here?" grumbled Mr. Cookiepants.

"This is going to be so worth it," I said. "We have proof!"

"Of what?" asked Mr. Cookiepants.

Pasha raised our tightly rolled evidence tube over his head again and shouted his answer: "That we have nothing to fear but fear itself!"

Chapter 60

"Follow us, please," I told the cats clustered around our stump.

"Single file," said Poop. "The path into the pet cemetery is kind of narrow."

"But the woods are so dark and deep!" whined a tortoiseshell. "Are there miles to go before I sleep?"

"The graveyard is actually pretty close by," I assured him. And then Poop and I led the forty-nine cats (Ermine did a quick tail count) deeper and deeper into the forest.

"I'm afraid of the dark!" a cat traipsing behind us shouted.

"Don't be!" cried Little Luigi, who was bringing up the rear of the line. "It's just what the world looks like when they switch off the sun."

"I'm still afraid that Scaredy Cat will find out what we're doing," mumbled Mr. Cookiepants. "He doesn't like cats clumping together, except at his rallies. He could banish us all to the woods!"

"Don't worry," said the crusty stray cat leader, K, with a laugh. "You'd only have to spend a night or two with us. You're so plump and juicy, the coyotes would gobble you down in an instant."

"There are coyotes out here?" another cat peeped. "I'm afraid of coyotes!"

"Yes," I said, "we all have our fears. Things and creatures we're afraid of. And fear can be very powerful. It can stop us from doing what we want to do. Fear can also lead to the quest for power. Because if we have power, we think that power will help us overcome our fears."

"That's what Scaredy Cat is doing," added Poop. "Making all the cats on Strawberry Lane tremble in fear so he doesn't have to be so afraid himself."

"What?" scoffed Mr. Cookiepants. "Scaredy Cat isn't afraid of anything. Are you seriously suggesting that he is, secretly, some sort of fraidycat?"

"Yes," I said. "That's exactly what I'm seriously suggesting."

We trooped into the pet cemetery and got everybody organized in a semicircle around Ebenezer's mausoleum.

"Um, why are we stopping here?" someone asked.

"So," I told her, "you can, once and for all, lay your fears of Scaredy Cat to rest."

"Huh? How is standing in a circle around a cat named Ebenezer's tomb going to do that?"

"Simple," said Poop. "Ebenezer and Scaredy Cat are one and the same!"

I unfurled our photograph and showed the hushed crowd what Poop had found on that lamp table upstairs in the creepy cottage. Not another portrait or oil painting of Ebenezer. This was a simple photograph of Mrs. von Bumbottom posing with her cat.

"Behold Ebenezer and Mrs. von Bumbottom!"

Chapter 61

All the oil paintings and portraits of Ebenezer hanging on the walls of that upstairs bedroom?

Not a single one of them was as powerful as the slightly crinkled photograph my friend Pasha finally showed to our audience. It was a somewhat faded snapshot of an elderly woman cradling a frowning cat in her lap. You could see the fear in the cat's eyes. The hate and anger in the old woman's.

"That's Ebenezer?" said Ermine.

"Yep," I said. "And Mrs. von Bumbottom."

"Ebenezer looks exactly like Scaredy Cat," Ermine continued. "Same markings. Same eyes."

"That scary old lady looks like an owl," remarked K.

"She sure does," added Pasha.

"An angry old owl," said Mr. Cookiepants, shivering slightly.

Pasha nodded. "Indeed she does. I suspect that's why Scaredy Cat never came into our backyard once Mr. Wilde posted a solar-powered plastic owl back there."

"Scaredy Cat was too afraid," I added. "He thought the owl with the bobbing head was the ghost of the evil Mrs. von Bumbottom come back to haunt him! One ghost scaring another ghost!"

"Ghosts?" said K. "Let me get this straight. Scaredy Cat used to be Ebenezer? The ghost of this Ebenezer cat *is* Scaredy Cat? The cat that's terrorized every single feline on both sides of the golf course for all these years is nothing but a Halloween spook?"

"Precisely!" said Pasha.

"Here lies Ebenezer," I declared. "And here also lies Scaredy Cat. They are one and the same."

"Except one's a ghost," said Little Luigi. "Right? That's what you said earlier."

"Correct," said Pasha. "Scaredy Cat is nothing more than a restless spirit. In fact, I almost feel sorry for him. The ghost of Ebenezer is trapped here on Strawberry Lane, a cul-de-sac with no exit, because he's too afraid to move on to whatever comes next."

Once again, I would've snapped my fingers if I'd had them. "That's how come he can walk through doors and hedges and magically appear in a *poof* of smoke! I've seen ghosts do all that inside the TV. He also has that ghoulish green glow. And can float..."

"He doesn't smell very fresh, either," added Mr. Cookiepants, waving his paw under his nose like he just smelled last week's sushi. "I often regretted sitting in the front row at his rallies..."

"Scaredy Cat's reign of fear is over," announced Pasha. "We know what he is. A ghost. A spirit. And once you have that knowledge? Well, knowledge always defeats fear."

"Pasha's right," I said. "On TV, ghosts never really hurt anybody. They just scare human beings into hurting themselves."

Suddenly, a bone-chilling "meowwww" filled the night air.

Forty-nine cats puffed up their tails and ballooned out their fur coats. Forty-nine cats whipped their heads around, looking for the source of that terrifying, yowling cry.

"Up here, you fools."

He was back.

Scaredy Cat.

Chapter 62

I perched myself on the peak of my mausoleum.

It was a very dramatic entrance, if I do say so myself, which I do, because I AM THE SCAREDY CAT!

I made my orange eyes glow like embers in a smoldering fire. It's one of my best tricks. The smoldering eyes.

Then I hissed and sent sizzling spittle spewing out of my mouth as if it were a spray bottle filled with vinegar. I pawed at the air with curled claws out, the way a lion might if it were as fierce as me.

"I'm so glad you all could join me out here in my graveyard, a place where many of you will soon be sleeping inside old shoe boxes if you dare defy me. But let's pretend this is just another one of MY rallies, shall we? Let's say you all came out to the woods well after midnight because you were eager to hear more pearls of wisdom ooze forth from my lips."

I added a little more blistering spittle to the lips line. A real stone sizzler.

But, for some reason, it wasn't working. None of the cats below were quaking or trembling in fear.

I suddenly wished I hadn't chosen to wear Mrs. von Bumbottom's favorite Christmas costume. The angel look was rather humiliating. Especially after I had been such a devil.

I looked down at all the upturned cat faces. Many were shaking their heads, wondering why they had ever been afraid of me.

One of them, the cat named Pasha, was looking up at me with pity in his eyes.

"It's okay, Ebenezer," said his little friend, Poop. "You don't have to pretend to be a Scaredy Cat anymore."

"You wanted us to find this photograph, didn't you?" said Pasha, the brainy one. "You're tired of being stuck in this rut. You're tired of being afraid.

You want to say good-bye to Mrs. von Bumbottom and move on, don't you."

My shoulders sagged. I heaved out a sigh. I took off my wire halo.

"It is exhausting," I admitted. "Stoking all this rage? Making my eyeballs glow? Constantly coming up with mean and nasty magic tricks? It's wearing me out. And, if I'm being honest, I'm sick and tired of Strawberry Lane. This was where I was most miserable. I don't want to be stuck here for all eternity! I want to move on!"

PASHA

Chapter 63

All the rage and anger had drained out of Scaredy Cat's eyes, to be replaced by tears.

Happy tears.

He looked relieved. Like he had just faced his worst fears and survived. Well, as much as a dead spirit can be said to survive.

The cat named Ebenezer had lived his life in fear. Now he realized he didn't have to do the same thing in death.

"I could never be perfect enough for Mrs. von Bumbottom," Ebenezer told us as he slipped out of his ridiculous Christmas costume. It disappeared with a nearly silent *FWOOF*. The tinsel-wrapped halo, too.

Scaredy Cat was no longer snarling and mysterious. He was just Ebenezer. A big ball of fluff who in life, like all cats, had deserved a much happier home.

"I lived my whole life in fear. Constantly worried what I might do to make Mrs. von Bumbottom angry at me. Putting on costumes to make her happy. Obeying all the proper cat rules. But there was no way to please her. She treated me worse than she treated her son, Loach."

"And that was pretty horrible," said Lenny.

The ghost of Ebenezer nodded. "I didn't hate Loach for hating me. We should've been friends, I suppose. We shared a common tormentor. We could've shared our fears. If we'd done that, maybe we could've done something about them. Instead, we both remained locked inside our own cages, where the bars were forged out of fear. Anyway, when death finally came for me, I wasn't ready to move on. I was afraid that, one day, Mrs. von Bumbottom would move on, too. I didn't want to face her wrath and fury for all eternity on the other side. So I chose to stay here, in this realm, and make others afraid. I vowed to do to them what had been done to me. It made me feel better. Stronger. I acted the way I wish I could've acted when I was alive. I wish I could've made Mrs. von Bumbottom tremble and quake in fear the way she made me tremble and quake. The way I made all of you...well, most of you...tremble and quake."

Suddenly, Ebenezer's eyes widened, as if he were seeing something far off on the horizon.

"But now I'm ready to go. I don't have to be afraid of what waits on the other side. Fear is something we create in our minds. It's the greatest illusion, the scariest trick of all. But if we create it, we can also conquer it!"

"Ebenezer?" I said.

"Yes, Pasha?"

"I hope you rest in peace. You deserve to."

"Thank you."

He started to slowly fade away.

"So long, Ebenezer!" shouted Ermine. "We're gonna miss you. Not!"

Ebenezer smiled.

And then he disappeared.

Forever.

Poop

Chapter 64

Of course, the house cats and even the stray cats didn't one hundred percent believe what happened that night in the pet cemetery.

To tell you the truth, I'm not sure I believed it, either.

But Pasha sure did.

"We faced our fear and, in so doing, conquered it."

Day after day, week after week, Scaredy Cat didn't reappear.

We went back to being cats! Lazing in the sunshine, chasing fur mice, gobbling down dinner, being happy, purring like motorboats.

Ermine was a constant visitor to our backyard.

"So that's the owl, huh?" she asked. "The one Scaredy Cat thought was Mrs. von Bumbottom?"

"Indeed," said Pasha.

Ermine sighed.

In fact, she sighed whenever Pasha said "indeed" or quoted Shakespeare. She thought my housemate had a "beautiful brain."

"You should come live with us," I suggested to her.

"What?"

"It's clear that you and Pasha belong together."

"Yes, please, Ermine," pleaded Pasha. "Give up your wild ways. Come live with us at the Wildes'!"

"Oh, no," Ermine said. "I couldn't do that."

"Why not?" I asked.

"I'm afraid. The Wildes wouldn't want me. I'm a misfit. I only have one eye."

"And," said Pasha, wiggling his ears, "*I* only have eyes for you!"

"Would you hurry up and say yes?" I said to Ermine. "Otherwise, Pasha's going to keep saying sappy stuff, which might make me lose my lunch."

"B-b-but..."

I could hear the fear in her voice. The fear of rejection.

"Hey," I said, "what did we just learn about fear?"

Ermine thought. "That it only exists in our heads."

"Exactly. So come on. Be the stray that followed us home. I'm pretty sure the Wildes will adopt you. Even if they don't, you won't have to fear what they might do or say because they will have already done or said it!"

Pasha looked at me. "Poop? Did you, by chance, also spend your early days with a wise and learned professor?"

"Nah. Just these past few months with you. But I'm a fast learner."

And the Wildes? Well, they fall in love with cats, fast.

In under a week, Ermine was officially the third cat in our happy little family. The Wildes even threw her a "homecoming" party.

When things settled down, the three of us gave ourselves a new mission.

"There are probably other Scaredy Cats out there," said Pasha. "Ghostly spirits, roaming around. Terrorizing their neighbors."

"Because they're secretly afraid themselves, right?" said Ermine.

"Exactly. We should do out there what we did here on Strawberry Lane. We should rid the land of Scaredy Cats, one neighborhood at a time!"

Pasha, of course, was right.

We were going to put an end to fear, once and for all!

Well, at least in our little corner of the world.

Ermine

Chapter 65

Let me just say how great it is living at the Wildes'.

BTW: a lot of my forest friends went back to their old homes or found new ones!

But I got the best!

And not just because Pasha lives here, too. And Poop. She's cool. Like the sister I never had or even knew I wanted. Also, there's fresh, wholesome food. Twenty-four-seven. And clean water. And warm beds that the human beans can plug into the wall to make them even warmer.

But we still had that mission.

It was time to start ridding our world of Scaredy Cats. So one morning, after the Wildes had given us our rubs and hugs and chin scratches and taken off on their own various adventures, I led the way to the Feeding Grounds.

"Where's that?" asked Pasha and Poop.

"Beyond the woods, on the far side of the golf course. It'll be quite a hike, but, well, a few of my friends from the northern end of the forest eat out of the dumpsters there. And if there is a Scaredy Cat lurking in the shadows…"

"Say no more," said Pasha gallantly (which is kind of how he said everything).

So off we went. I led the way. It took us a little over an hour, but soon we were in the land of roaring tires and traffic.

"That's what Lenny calls the highway," I told my new friends. "Human beans drive their vehicles on it and then pull off to buy stuff."

"Aha!" said Pasha, reading a sign posted on a blocky building. "That's the restaurant where the Wildes pick up many of their take-home meals."

"Yeah," I said. "Lenny told us this is a strip mall. There are three restaurants, a nail parlor, and a place that sells phone gadgets. The dumpsters out back? Behind the restaurants? I hear it's delish! An all-you-can-eat buffet of table scraps and fish on its way to going bad."

Pasha chuckled as we scampered around back to the service entrances and rolling trash bins. "This reminds me of my childhood in St. Petersburg."

"The one in Russia," said Poop, with an eye roll. "Not Florida."

"Yes," sighed Pasha. "There's nothing quite like the scent of—"

He didn't get to finish that thought.

Because a monstrous, furless beast—what human beans call a Sphynx cat—appeared from behind the nearest dumpster.

"Oh, good, good, good," said the wrinkled Scaredy Cat, hissing. "I've been expecting you three. My plan, my very special plan, is to turn you all into alley cats. Mee-OWWWWW! Now then, in this parking lot, there are a few rules…"

We just looked at her.

And then we laughed.

And then we laughed louder!

This new Scaredy Cat didn't scare us.

Because we wouldn't let it!

GET YOUR PAWS ON THE

HILARIOUS DOG DIARIES SERIES!

Read the Middle School series

Visit the **Middle School world** on the Penguin website
to find out more! **www.penguin.co.uk**

ALSO BY JAMES PATTERSON

MIDDLE SCHOOL BOOKS

The Worst Years of My Life (*with Chris Tebbetts*)
Get Me Out of Here! (*with Chris Tebbetts*)
My Brother Is a Big, Fat Liar
(*with Lisa Papademetriou*)
How I Survived Bullies, Broccoli, and
Snake Hill (*with Chris Tebbetts*)
Ultimate Showdown (*with Julia Bergen*)
Save Rafe! (*with Chris Tebbetts*)
Just My Rotten Luck (*with Chris Tebbetts*)
Dog's Best Friend (*with Chris Tebbetts*)
Escape to Australia (*with Martin Chatterton*)
From Hero to Zero (*with Chris Tebbetts*)
Born to Rock (*with Chris Tebbetts*)
Master of Disaster (*with Chris Tebbetts*)
Field Trip Fiasco (*with Martin Chatterton*)

DOG DIARIES SERIES

Dog Diaries (*with Steven Butler*)
Happy Howlidays! (*with Steven Butler*)
Mission Impawsible (*with Steven Butler*)
Curse of the Mystery Mutt (*with Steven Butler*)
Camping Chaos! (*with Steven Butler*)

THE I FUNNY SERIES

I Funny (*with Chris Grabenstein*)
I Even Funnier (*with Chris Grabenstein*)
I Totally Funniest (*with Chris Grabenstein*)
I Funny TV (*with Chris Grabenstein*)
School of Laughs (*with Chris Grabenstein*)
The Nerdiest, Wimpiest, Dorkiest I Funny Ever
(*with Chris Grabenstein*)

For more information about James Patterson's novels,
visit www.penguin.co.uk